1/9/20

For Jimmy, the o[illegible] rich, handsome and [illegible] Hudson is responsible for this book [illegible] knew where Ocilla (Kasoris) until he broke the lid there with his challenge to the Judge's ~~stat~~ shut up order to all within hearing of Irwin County.

EVIL COMES A CALLIN

Her sister and in fact the entire village refused to talk to me about the Kase! Anyway here we are so enjoy it.

Regards,

Glynn AKA K.G. WATSON

112 Raven Rdg
Maggie Valley, NC 28751

EVIL COMES A CALLIN

FROM PARADISE TO HELL

K. G. Watson

Palmetto Publishing Group
Charleston, SC

Evil Comes a Callin

First Edition

Printed in the United States

ISBN-13: 978-1-64111-262-8
ISBN-10: 1-64111-262-X

ACKNOWLEDGMENTS

I want to acknowledge my old friend and partner, Vernon J. Welch, who provided me with the challenge that began the project, the help I needed when my creativity became challenged and the motivation to see it through. I also want to thank Catherine Burr for helping me make this manuscript readable.

CONTENTS

INTRODUCTION

Our mystery in this publication develops in Southwest Georgia, a vast farming area of some 45 counties. The identification of towns and parties in this work is fictional and not built upon any person, alive or deceased. The crimes herein are foreign to this large land of agricultural production; the populace derived from earlier settlements in the 18th and 19th Centuries by English and Scotch immigrants. Many of these had fought in the Revolutionary War and most of their G G Fathers fought in the Civil War, 1860-65. A land of small towns, many sparsely settled; a few counties having populations of less than 1000.Our heroine herein is a bright, pretty, vivacious young lady, who moves to the town of Prosperity at the age of 15; enjoying High School there before attending Mercer University, Macon, Ga.; graduating with a degree in History; then returning to her roots to teach High School.

Later, she obtains her Masters' Degree from Valdosta College and begins teaching at the Worth County Community College, in addition to her High School job in Prosperity. Morgan's life revolves around this town from her first win at a Beauty Pageant in Highschool to Mercer, where she wins other Beauty-Talent Pageants. She remains the lovely, compassionate lady that she was prior to her triumphs in the contests; liked by all; she was careful about her relationships, seeking the perfect mate for herself. This was very unrewarding for her as fate seemed to deny her the successes in relationships that all the young sought. As she approached 30 years of age, her thoughts remained on marriage, children and a wonderful mate. All of these were within her grasp but eluded her for reasons unknown. She did not share her inner thoughts with others, retaining these melancholy desires within. At times the words of "THE GREAT PRETENDER" a popular tune in the '60s by The Platters; applied to her; "she was lonely but no one could tell". She threw herself totally into her teaching, educating many, not only with subject matter but, in the traits of confidence, social skills and determination. Her efforts with men were mixed but, one would think that, with her looks and talents, it would be smooth sailing. Was she too superior for local males; tied by tradition or convenience to those residing in the immediate area? We'll never know; at Mercer she did not date, being entranced by Bud Carter, her first and last love.

It seems, at times, that one having looks, education and a sparkling personality; might have some degree of insecurity, hidden from the world but, always with the individual. Is this trait perhaps inflicted to, slow down the host, inhibiting her from 'overrunning her headlights'? Or is it nature's way of enlightening her on the uncertainties of life? Whatever the reason, many wrestle with the pain of having their confidence curtailed, as this 'self-doubt' conducts mental engagement with their normal confidence.

Many ladies perhaps, while thinking about Morgan; thought that her life-style, was perfect; they with one or more children, were almost totally occupied with household and care of toddlers. It's easy to see both views of the pitcher; one, a wrinkled crone and the other, a picture of a beautiful young girl. Many times, in life, it's easy to depreciate our places in the universe by unrealistic and slanted observations of another's life.

Most ladies admired her for her character and opportunities with her choices of swains. Her life was active, full and promising, until 22 Oct 2005 when she disappeared from her home and town. There was an 11year period when she was sought constantly without success. The search was never over but there was nothing to invigorate those seeking her fate. Only in the final chapter is it revealed what actually happened to her, one of the most wrenching secrets in the history of Georgia criminality. The intense pain suffered by family and friends of the missing lady; just not knowing of her cause for departing the area; over such a long period of eleven years; resulted in casualties in the family and among acquaintances. But what can one do except live a melancholy life?

CHAPTER I:
NEW ENVIRONS

When Morgan found out about the move from Ashburn to Prosperity in mid-June 1990, she was, at the least, disappointed. Ashburn was on an interstate highway and, easy to navigate on Interstate 75, either North or South. From her scant knowledge of Prosperity, it was in the sticks, in the farmland of Worth County; not exactly the most desirable place on the universe. There was just her and her parents as her older sister, Marsha, was a Junior at Mercer University, Macon, Ga. "Darn it", Morgan exclaimed, as she thought of leaving her Ashburn friends AND moving to Tim-Buc-Two. And there was no appeal from this decision as her Father had gotten a promotion out of the move and likely, they could have a larger house. Who could she talk to about this disastrous move? Actually, no-one around here had ever spent any time in Prosperity so it was a new adventure or disaster, depending on the point of view. So by 1 July, it was wheels off the ground, Prosperity the next stop.

It wasn't a long trip BUT the furniture still had to go by moving van, be packed neatly, then unpacked carefully when arriving at our new house, complete with wide front porch, shade trees and ceiling fans on the front porch and in each room of the house. It was white with a broad lawn and sweet shrubs around the front porch. The house was so big that it appeared to be a senior citizens' home. The telephones were already installed, just waiting for me to call my friends.

Arriving later the van parked adjacent to the front of the house, and the men carefully unloaded each piece, placing it as my Mother directed. My bedroom was across the hall from my Parents room, shaded by a mature pecan tree, to shield me from the hot sun. It wasn't entirely air conditioned BUT had a number of window units to cut down on the Georgia humidity. Finally, the unloading was completed, the van departed and we sat down to catch our breaths. Well, here I am, isolated from my friends and popular spots known to me. My first night, mused Morgan, was a mixed blessing; "Yes, I liked my new room, the spacy home and the grounds BUT what do I do for a social life?" I thought, " my life is over, no more peanut boilings, cane grindings or rides on the hay wagons; my trophies for the contests will just gather dust without any additions to the numbers."

Sleep did come to Morgan that night AND the next day she met the other teenagers on the block; another 9th grader, a Sophomore, Alice, and two Juniors, Bobby and Bud, both athletes. There was life after Ashburn, Morgan realized, as she shared her past with this small group. She began to realize as they conversed that there was little difference in the lives of those of Turner County and Worth County. In fact, her social calendar was filling up already. Prosperity had onc thing that Ashburn lacked, a movie theatre, vanishing from most towns but stalwart in Worth Co. So the films were dated; the best actors/actresses were still in them, giving their superb performances. The 'dress' was top notch, the ladies dressed 'fit to kill', referring to the Southernism speaking of the tradition of 'always' insuring that the deceased was laid out in the best attire to be found. Strange? Not in the South; if the relatives had no classy garments to supply to the mortuary, then the negligee for the ladies AND the coat, shirt and tie were furnished by the mortuary (at a premium, of course).

Most of the teenagers were familiar with parochial statements and rites, so there was no necessity to explain the intricacies of Southern wakes, burials and internments I.e.to return to the cemetery later in the day to retrieve the cards for the donors of the flowers. Someone had to take care of the administrative details completing the matter. And of course, the undertakers bill must be settled prior to the service. The name 'wake' was a lingering remembrance when medicine was not precise and at times, the alleged deceased would rise up in the coffin, not dead yet. In order to prevent cardiac arrest among the mourners,ladies would sit in the living room with the casket, watching for any twitch from it as the gentlemen sat in the kitchen sampling Jim Beam, etc., telling stories of a man while extolling the virtues of a lady deceased. All orderly and per the mores of the jurisdiction.

Morgan frolicked that morning, returning at noon for her sandwich and milk; many households prepared a big meal for mid-day as the yeoman returned from the field, hungry and thirsty. His routine was to eat, drink his fill of iced tea and then lie down on the porch or on the floor with a feather pillow to seek the land of nod. In no more than 120 minutes, maybe less, he arose like Lazarus, took his tractor in hand, assuming his task of planting, weeding or breaking ground. The farm equipment was becoming so intricate that one needed a mechanical engineer's degree to get the most horsepower from it.

You remember how the steamy days of Summer seemed to go as fast as molasses pouring from a frozen jug. The comments "is it still Monday? when is my date? My bathing suit is wet, might I buy another?" My Mother disliked the Summer break as much as we did; but think of NO homework, late sleeping, midweek dates or get togethers. I had transformed these-past few months from a middle schooler to a big Freshwoman vying with the know-it-alls to see who learns the secrets of the universe first. Morgan let her thoughts float..."wonder what courses I can take this Fall? Accidentally, she spoke question out loud and Mitzy, a neighbor, spoke, "exactly the same the whole class takes, reading, writing AND adding". Morgan, "no civics, no science, no physical training?" Mitzy, " we will have some as filler but literature will be featured as rea ding, penmanship and expressive writing as writing and so on". Morgan, "so there is light at the end of the tunnel?" M "surely, we are likely to be challenged our Fall Quarter but I view us as the best and brightest in Prosperity". Morgan " thanks for your vote of confidence; now for more important matters, like swimming".

Morgan "where do we swim here?" Mitzi "the pool at the park or the Flint River a mile or so from here. Take your choice." Morgan, "the river sounds so dangerous, is it?" Mitzi, "it can be, we don't get out into the rapid water but Bud is a Red Cross Lifeguard." Morgan, thinking out loud," maybe I'd better try the pool until I get my skills into shape; is that OK?" Mi." Good idea, Morg; we'll pick you up at 1245."

The group scattered to gobble down a sandwich and the standard iced tea; unless their Father was a farmer, but most lived on their farms; and needed his calories and midday rest. Morgan knew all about these mores as Turner Co (Ashburn) was as Worth, completely consumed by the production of foodstuffs and some tobacco. The latter was being phased out with only a select few given an allotment. She knew about the allotments and the unfairness of them. For instance, she tallied in her head the No 1 wrong about these...the allotment went with the land AND if the land was sold, so was the allotment. A new farmer could not obtain an allotment for sandspurs UNLESS he bought one(unlikely) or rented one yearly (the usual). So the active farmers had a monopoly on the allotments. Morgan thought, "how unfair; it relegated the newer farmers to crops like corn, not strictly controlled, truck crops (vegetables) and soybeans (tough to make it with these without gobs of soil". Morgan was not only a very pretty Lass but an brain also, figuring out the unfairness of the USDA, the boss man of our yeomen. Oh well, Morgan thought, "this cool swim will ease my mental gymnastics."

Right on time several came for Morgan, who, as all, had her suit, a modest one-piece(yellow) on. The dressing rooms at the pool were awful so it was better to come ready to plunge in. They had a minor fee of 35 cents for anyone over 10, but Morgan forgot her purse. Bud said, " Morgan, I'll take care of it and you can furnish the lemon aide when we finish the swim." Morg looked at Bud who was smiling like a jackass eating briars; she smiled saying, "yes, Master, may I shine your shoes?". Bud was surprised and unable to respond quickly, finally mumbling, "I only have flipflops on". End of repartee or repost.

They all dove in, the girls wearing bathing caps for hair protection, since weekly dating was in for the summer. It did look funny to the boys but they knew the reason. One or two of the girls had two-piece suits on, livening up the scenery; Times were changing here in the farm country. Morgan had one also but was moving slowly into the waters of Prosperity; no need to excite anyone. Morgan was 5'4", about 117, blue eyes and very dark hair. She had a nice figure with everything in the right places; not too much but just as Goldilocks said of Baby Bear's porridge.......just right. This was before the breast enhancement/reduction rage hit the country so girls had WHAT they had; no silicone to sag later, spoiling the entire figure.

Naturally, the boys tried a bit of hand pumping of the water to hit the girls BUT not too hard or too often; these were their prospective dates for the summer; why make them angry over stupid tricks? After 2-3 hours of sun and cool H2O, as with all teenagers, it was time to move on and leave the pool to the younger set. They loaded up, Morgan next to Bud, the athlete, and headed for the Drive-In for a milkshake or soda. Morgan thought, "darn, I don't have any money, should I lean on Bud, the 6'0',180 pound Q Back for Prosperity, for sustenance?" Well, Morgan was in a bind but Bud was right there with his wallet to fill the bill. He decided not to tease her this time as he thought that she was a Fox, and his type. He didn't know exactly what or whom a Fox was but likely the female was very attractive, spoke softly, dressed well and, hopefully, liked athletes. He thought that "normally they are older but this girl is 'so fine' that she can be accelerated to the head of the class, any class." "So, quit the horseplay, Mr. Bud, NOW" thought the Q Back. He politely asked, "Morgan what would you like?". She said in her softest voice, "How about a chocolate shake, Bud, with 2 straws?" Bud didn't bat an eye, ordering this for her, but a bit uncertain about the straws. It arrived and he handed it to Morgan along with the straws. She took her time, peeling the paper cover from one, then sticking it in the giant cup; the other she peeled half way, t hen handed Bud the paper end. He could hardly contain his pleasure but did complete its uncovering, inserting it into the shake. Morgan smiled, saying, "Bud, I knew that you'd help me with this gigantic shake". Bud just smiled. The two of them with the straws exiting on opposite sides of the 'shake', looking at each other, resembled one of the paintings by, both smiling; others oblivious to the 'happening'. Soon Morgan arrived at her new 'digs', exited as did Bud, walking her to her door. Not much time for them to converse and there had no opportunity for an exchange of phone or cell numbers. Bud," Morgan I really enjoyed your company; welcome to Prosperity." She "Bud, you've really welcomed me; you might know that I've been in the 'dumps' for weeks, worrying about what I might find here. Leaving a comfortable place even though this is only 40 miles from Ashburn, is unnerving to a teen. You and the group have taken the edge off my nervousness so thank you". Bud, "like to call you soon, may I have your phone number?". Morgan, "sure, its 294 331 4156 AND I do have an extension in my room. Ill be busy each afternoon and night helping my Mother straighten out the house BUT this weekend is open ". Him, " Think on Friday night; we might just cook out at my house". Morgan, "call me and we'll discuss it". Him, "great, talk to you later".

She slowly went into the house, her Mother greeting her,"did you enjoy the young people this afternoon?". She responded, "they are great guys and gals; I believe that I will fit in nicely in Prosperity; I can't wait for school to start". Mother, "I'm so pleased at that; your Father and I had been worried about moving you at this time in your life; but it is such an opportunity for him to advance. Your sister will be finishing Mercer this year and another change for her as she seeks a job; The economy is not bad but so many are completing college and grad school, that the competition might be stiff. She and her friend, the soon to be Doctor, might be joining permanently, before too long. Life is full of changes and you within 2 years or so will be selecting a college, whether Mercer, Valdosta State, Ga. Southwestern, Ga. Southern or elsewhere". Morgan, "I haven't thought about it but UGA is on my mind; not seriously but just with me". Mother, " I'll need you to help me each night this week beginning now with the house". Morgan just smiled as she went to her room.

She thought about this afternoon and the ease with which she made friends; whew, she was relieved BUT does Bud have a girlfriend? If so, where is she? Well, if there is a friend, she will be on the scene promptly; Bud didn't act like one who is cutting out on his girlfriend but who knows? I could ask Mitzy or one of the other girls BUT why? I don't need to be nervous or afraid; I think that Bud would give me a sign if there was a 3rd in the picture. Time will tell. I spent the rest of the afternoon helping Mother put away the linens, pots and pans, books, records and the balance of the packed goods. Tomorrow we'll tackle the wardrobes, except for size and weight, are not a problem. I hoped that my dress clothes wouldn't be so wrinkled that they needed dry cleaning; that costs a ton even in 1991. We really got with it that night and after showering, my exhausted body hit the bed. The Land of Nod was not far I didn't wake early but when I did around 0800, I was so hungry that I could eat shoe leather. I smelled coffee and bacon, enough for a tired Worth Country girl.

Dad had come in late from the mill, slept briefly and gone back early. He wanted a quick start on his new job and that seemed wise. In this area, peanuts were the 'gold' to be mined; the procedures had changed from earlier times. Some time ago, the farmers cut poles 6"X8" called stack poles to place in the fields, after affixing pieces of wood to them to hold the peanuts to dry. The peanuts had been plowed up but still required labor with pitchforks to move the product to the poles. Finally someone decided that just plowing them up with the nuts to the sun, could do as well. Farm laborers were getting scarce and labor-saving methods and machinery were in vogue. Voila.

The peanut mills had incorporated large dryer operations so there was now more profit in this valuable product. SW Georgia shipped peanut butter, salted peanuts, peanuts in mixtures as well as some still in the shells to all parts of the U.S. as well as South America and Orient. Everybody liked peanuts, raw, cooked, parched and boiled. The soil in this large area of Georgia was what is called 'pebble soil' having little red tiny rocks in the sandy soil. This soil assisted the peanut vine to spread between the rows to form an almost complete growth linking the 2 rows. When the middle closed in, the product was just about ready to 'dig'.

Morgan washed her face, headed for the dining room, from which the scents emanated. Her Mother had already eaten so she sat, filled her plate with grits (of course), bacon, fruit,adding a large glass of orange juice. Even though she was 'starving' she said a short 'grace' as the family always did. Without a companion she mowed down the country breakfast, wiped her attractive face with a napkin, and went to dress for work. In a flash she was with her Mother getting her work assignments,

I.e. fold and put the linens away in the hall closet. Morgan had never seen so many towels, hand towels, BR mats, etc. She dove in, moving with nimbleness to do her job. Her Mother was just as intense and before long, it was noon and Dad would be home soon. Then he came in, inquiring about their progress and viewing all the paper and boxes. Mother fixed our lunch and did sit a short time as we ate. The respite was over too soon; Dad went back to the mill and we tackled the china, dishes, nick- nacks and miscellaneous; thank goodness for a large dishwasher to churn out the clean glass items. The afternoon drug along but at 4:30 P she exited the work area to prepare for Mr. Bud; she felt so gritty that a tub bath sounded good to her. She eased in, enjoying every minute of it, just thinking about how her life was changing so rapidly. After she pampered herself so much, she exited to her room to determine her attire for this important event. Generally, in her estimation, dresses were out except for church from June to Sept; instead it was shorts, mid- style or cutoffs. Morgan thought and came to a conclusion, shorts and a light blouse or T-shirt. They were going to see her legs sometime and tonight was just as well. She had some green shorts and a white blouse that hugged her chest. She tried both on, looking in the mirror to check herself. She looked good so why not.

She was ready at 5:45 P, nervous a bit but confidant. Right on time, Bud pulled up in his Dad's Ragtop, called a convertible by some. Aqua with a white top, naturally already down. He rang the doorbell and Morgan invited hm in to meet her Mother and Dad. He was charming as most Southern boys from good families were. Morgan did the introductions, small talk for a brief period and then up, up and away. Of course Bud opened the car door for her, looking at her legs all the while.

Bud drove slowly and the conversation lagged a bit until Morgan poked Nit a bit. She inquired about his house," do you live in town?" Bud, "on the outskirts, the town was here when we arrived, with little land left to build on; there was a new subdivision opening on the Sylvester highway with several acres for each site". M..." describe your house for me". B..."I think that it is an English Tudor." Morgan..."that sounds like Macon or Columbus; any brothers or sisters?" B"One sister, married and a brother at UGA". M..."like me, my sister is finishing Mercer next year; majoring in business and music". By this time, Bud was turning into his driveway with this beautiful home right here". He stopped, opened my door and we went to the front door. It was opened and his Father and Mother greeted me; Bud introduced me and we chatted briefly before he escorted me to the backyard. A couple were already there so the introductions were done again.

I saw right away that almost all of the attendees were older than myself but that's still Ok. We all kidded around for a while as others straggled out to the area of the fire and grill. A colored man was taking care of everything so I knew that the meat wouldn't be burned and Bud could be attentive to me. He did have manners and so did the other boys, mostly in the 11th Grade. The girls were a mixture of 10thand 11th grades, the latter already talking about colleges and universities. UGA was very popular in this area, even if it is a hike from Worth County. Several of the locals, according to Bud, had played football at UGA. He didn't indicate if that was his desire.

Morgan "I listened mostly as the boys ragged one another about in and everything, as the girls talked about college, vacations to come, shopping in Albany, the only town of any size in SW Georgia; the closest place to shop was Cordele, about 30 miles up highway 32. Then someone said, "why do we have so many small counties in this area?" Good question and Bud scooped it up, " it started around 1900 when people began to resist driving a buggy or wagon to the Couty site and it requiring a minimum of two days to be back home. Almost all had business at the Courthouse at some time and the two- day absence from the fields really hurt the farmer or anyone. So, between 1905 and

1920, new counties were carved out of Worth, Dooly, Houston, and others. Now we have only 159 counties as two were incorporated into Fulton during the great Depression. The laws for combining counties now are so rigorous and, the opposition of the local populace is usually so strong that the politicos just leave these uneconomic situations to survive or not. There is a strong tendency for one politician to control these sparsely populated political creations."

Someone shouted, "Bravo for Bud".; another, "that's his longest utterance since he memorized our plays before a game". Morgan, "Bud, that's great; Georgia history in a nutshell; how did you learn this?". Bud, reluctantly, "Dad said that I needed to learn something, at least, about this large area of South Georgia, that certainly wouldn't be learned in school; I went to the library to research the current alignment and was surprised at the small populations of a number of our counties; some as few as 1200 or so, to support the courthouse 'gang' which usually brings in little revenue." Morgan, "why do they cling to this archaic system, Bud?" B "it's hard to say but I think that it's the fear of losing their voices and control over local governments". M. " will it ever change?" B. "probably not in our lifetimes". Morgan, "wow".

Someone said, "food's served" and it was. To describe the feast is too much but there were small tenderloins, roasted corn, fresh tomatoes, lightly garlicked bread and of course, iced tea. The boys asked each lady about her selections In order to retrieve her plate. Soon all were seated on the couches, easy chairs or edge of the patio, just plunging into this repast; the conversation dwindled as the jaws were occupied with other matters. Morgan thought, "these girls are eating; no holding back so why not me?" Her thought was, "I'm now in another venue so I must or should do as the Romans do; why pick at great cuisine?"

As we finished, Bud whispered to me, "let's take you through the house; they won't miss us." He took our plates of fine china, placed them on the serving table and we scooted to the house, remembered

Morgan. This house, while not massive, was adequate for any family, 4 bedrooms upstairs, 3 full baths, an office for Dad and, downstairs, a sewing room for his Mom, a formal dining room, a small breakfast room, a full bath (for cleanup after hunting), elegant living room and a Ladies half bath fixed as a boutique. Morgan was entranced as she took it all in.

Back with the gang, most just strolled the grounds, immaculate with the giant oaks with an occasional white pine or long leaf pine intermixed. The straw/needles from the pines served to mulch the outside house plants., conserving moisture and adding to the soil fertility. At least, that was Bud's take on it and I took it as the gospel. "In my estimation", Morgan opined, " this house, yard, grounds, all of it, was the epitome of the perfect country home". The others began softly saying their thanks and departing; naturally Bud waited until all had departed and then we left in the aqua convertible; it was only 12 minutes to my house so he drove slowly as I thought he, like myself, wanted to prolong the pleasure. Finally we got to my house; the parents tucked in, the small front light on, all awaiting me. Bud," Gee, Morg, this was something; I thought the cookout would be just a rerun of our usual outings. NOT so, your presence added a flavor, not often seen around Prosperity". Morgan. "Bud, this night is something to write about; the young people of this town surely know how to conduct themselves in a social setting and impresses me with their characters".

Bud lit up like a Christmas tree with ruddy cheeks and a smile like a hallo-ween pumpkin. Morgan responded with her impressive smile and flashing dark eyes; she knew how to be attentive, keeping her eyes on her date. "Time to say goodnight" said Bud; Morgan nodded but didn't want to go inside. Gently, he embraced her, not attempting to kiss her or hold her too long. Bud," great night, is it OK if I call you tomorrow?" Morgan, "you'd better not forget". He moved to the car, waving as he moved out.

Morgan went in the house, sat down and just reflected on the happenings in her life these past few days. She was growing up and he was a gentleman, not attempting to become more friendly than the occasion dictated. She liked that; so much for the over-emphasized custom (if it was) of the escort bussing his date the first night. She knew that she would have permitted it but why follow such a stale habit of the romance authors?".

She showered, still in a slight trance from the evening but humming to herself. Drying off, she looked in the mirror, saw this maturing lady with a smile, rosy cheeks and all. She said, "is this Morgan or a new Morgana? Whomever, she would enjoy her years here, growing in grace and understanding of these people of the land, the descendants of the English, who arrived in the early 19thCentury, either bond servants (until their debts were paid) or yeomen who yearned for the freedom of the Colonies. Georgia being the largest of the 13 original states, there was a surplus of tillable land, adequate water and a kind sunshine. None of these were readily available in England and that unreasonable King George still ruled the roost.

As Morgan recalled her history, a wave of pride came over her; these brave people coming from so far to an unknown land without much in the way of assets except for energy and wits. But with fortune, these might be adequate to master the forests and rivers of this largest state East of the Mississippi. Her PJs on, she got into bed, leaving the light on as she documented her adventures this in her new diary. When she might feel nostalgic, she could take out this 'secret' record, refreshing her memory. The sandman came and she gave up the ghost, sleeping as a child; her former status.

She awoke unsure of the time but cognizant that she was on the work detail for this AM. She jumped up, donned some shorts and a Tee and headed for the kitchen where she often ate when alone. Her Mother was already on the job as Morgan greeted her, " it was great last night; his home is English Tudor and the grounds are huge with ancient oaks and long leaf pine scattered around. Any breakfast left?" Mother "Yes, in the stove; also, there is sweet potato pie, your favorite as I recall and non-fattening". M "wow is it my birthday?" Mother "only your benefits for the move".

Eating like a bird, a condor, she topped it off with the pie, wonderful as usual. Then on to work that was necessary to get the house in order. Morgan put a scarf around her head to keep away some of the dust that needed vacuuming TODAY. She and Mom slaved for several hours cleaning this house; the windows outside were so high that we needed a utility man to finish them off. When Dad came home, he agreed and sent a lad from the mill over to help. This old house could look attractive with a few more strokes of the dust brush or vacuum. Lunch was brief but Dad told us about his office and personnel; the mill had a number of experienced hands making most tasks simple. The trick about the mill was to parcel out the jobs relating to peanuts over 111/2 months; closing for 2 weeks at the end of the Summer.

After lunch, it was back to the job; a large house is nice but more help is needed to keep it going. Dad said that he'd be on the lookout for a mature woman to be with us full time. Mom and Morgan gave a cheer.

This was Saturday night but Morgan's plans were to stay home; she needed to browse through her clothes, selecting those too young looking for disposal; the Church (Baptist) had an emergency clothing supply to serve the community; what better for these garments? It was a large leap from 8th to 9th grade and Morgan wanted to make the jump in one leap. She had to have a cell phone to stay in touch with her friends here and a few in Ashburn. So, the campaign started for the cell; how to approach Dad was priority 1.

Morgan was wise not to approach him before he hung his hat; she waited until he had read the newspaper (all 7 pages of it) and got the early news from Albany. Nothing critical so she just sat down with him, pretending to be interested in current events. He said nothing so she was quiet as a mouse. After the silence got to her, Morgan began by talking about the difficulty of communication in rural areas. Dad agreed and innocently asked her, “what will you do about it?” Morgan saw the trap but was too far into the game to retreat. She,” it might help you keep track of me if I had a cell phone”. Dad said, “and you might be able to let us know where you are occasionally”. Morgan bit her tongue and grabbed the bull, “ Dad I need the cell; I can call my friends in Ashburn and stay in touch with those here”. Dad, “is there a tower in the area; you know, of course, that you must be within 20 miles to get service”. Morgan nodded, not knowing anything at all about towers, power, service. “I ll check tonight by calling the radio stations and report to in the morning as to the feasibility of my having a cell”. He was cracking up by then as Morgan was tied in knots. Dad, “You can have the cell as there are towers around; just check the others and see how their plans work”. Morgan gave him a big hug.

Another chore scratched off for Missy; she was on a roll BUT she knew from experience that trouble could appear as a black cloud before a rainstorm. Like Scarlett O’Hara, she settled it by saying to herself ,”I’ll worry about that tomorrow”. She was still working but the heavy lifting was over; just the finishing up was left. Morgan was sick of this moving; not being able to find anything was irritating BUT the whole venture was certainly worth it. There was only 3 weeks left before school started so I needed a course review in order to plan my year. Often there are help aids for sale at bookstores that can get one off to a fast start.

Bud called, “football practice begins on 15 August; twice a day 21/2 hours each to get honed for Cordele, a recent powerhouse. My activities will be curtailed until we get in a regular game mode. To bed at 9 PM; morning practices at 0730.” Morgan, aghast, mumbled, “you mean that we can’t go out till Sept?” Bud, “we can go but any after dark is very brief; it hurts us all. Afternoons are fine but practice at 6:30 P chills that option". M "well, it is what it is; we'll work around it; we're not delaying our dates until football playoffs in November". Bud laughed, "you know that we will find our times and wear out our cells rather than suffer because of football". Bud had to go, "See yah Sugar". Did Morgan hear him correctly?" "SUGAR; that's stepping out".

The unravelling began; one step forward and two back; life isn't easy; just look at the 'cell' phone discussion. Morgan searched the next day for school aids; she was taking Trig, American History, Elementary Writing, Typing and Physical Ed; a nice lineup for the 9th. These challenges would require great dedication especially the Fall Quarter. Since Bud is out of circulation, except for the weekends, Morgan determined to study hard and make good grades. But Bud could for one thing take her to Sunday School and Church AND lunch OR eat at her house. Morgan wasn't scheming too much, was she?".

The days flew by as Morgan and her Mother looked for clothes for her; in Cordele, Sylvester (no), Tifton, an up and coming town, agricultural center for the area with a giant display at least once a year of equipment, cotton pickers, peanut gatherers and soybean pickers as well as any new products for the big four: corn, cotton, peanuts and soybeans. The labs were constantly turning out new products similar to the uses for the sweet potatoes, initiated by George W. Carver in Alabama laboratories. Who would have thought years ago that the lowly soybean would one day be on a bun passing as a hamburger?

The afternoon ran fast but I did have a break when Bud called. We talked generally until he got around to it...he was having a grill out tonight at his house for 10 or so young folks; he needed me there to meet others. Could she go and could I pick her up about 6 M; home by 10 P. Morgan had not dated as an 8th grader so this was her first time out. Her Mother agreed and she told Bud she'd see him at 6 P. Bud was ecstatic about this 'coup'. So was Morgan; in town only 4 days and already a date with Mr. Big, football, class officer, Beta Club, on and on. Morgan was walking on air the remainder of the day; why not? Back to the drudgery of clearing out the boxes; it was no longer fun but at least she could get off early for the cookout. When the clock hit 4:30 P, she departed for the bath to clean up for her date.

CHAPTER II: EASIN ALONG

The weather was horrible as in all of SW's 45 counties, going to the pool was a relief but it was difficult to find another girl to go as many were at Summer Camp, on a trip or working at one of the few jobs outside of farm work. It seemed that all or almost all High School Students needed to work and many had to help out the farmers. But for school clothing, cash is first in line. Credit cards as most use, charge a 4% or so fee that adds up. In this age, Morgan thought, "a HS boy had to have access to money or his future with the girls was extremely bleak.

Morgan wondered how her economic knowledge had grown so much in very short time BUT with maturity grew a need for more than a roof, meals and overalls. The football guys were unable to work due to the practices that drained them ;their social lives suffered when school began; the girls didn't really understand the mathematics of 0 plus 0 equals 0.

It finally arrived, the beginning of her 9th grade; Morgan checked in as a new student, needed a birth certificate, a transcript of her 8th grade performance, $7.50 for the lunchroom, $3 for a workbook for trig and then she was a Prosperity student. The cheerleader trials were the end of the week but Morgan felt that she didn't know enough about the girls and the school and passed. Football was the name of this school and it seemed that all were so wrapped up in it that other activities were in last place.

Morgan wore her newest clothes early on; she tried skirts and blouses that could be switched around. Her looks were so great that one wondered, "who would notice her clothes?". It is customary for an attractive lady to check out her competition; Morgan looked over the other 9th graders, finding her place in the hierarchy still secure. Like many ladies, Morgan wasn't confidant of her looks so this trial run was good for her. Finally, day one was over and all fled the building, like a covey of quail when frightened.

It was rushed but exciting this first week; football Friday night; Cordele here. The stadium was nice for a small town; even the Ladies room was decent (unusual for most Southern stadiums. Kk If this necessity was quality, the Ladies could enjoy the game, having a coke or two. Friday came, the pep rally was at 2 PM with the entire high school student body turned out. The cheerleaders attired in aqua and light black, led the team on the field, with the band sweating as those horns and drums sounded like a tribe from Africa. The Coach had a few words ten turned it over to Bud for the finale. He was up to it "most of you guys were with us last year in Cordele when each of them excepting the water boy scored. Gentlemen, to be frank, they kicked our country asses. It was humiliating AND we are all dedicated to getting even. If you are not, leave your uniform in your locker; we can't carry any half-way athletes on this journey. I will try to stick to offense BUT if defense needs some help, I'll be there. I promise you 120% effort and I expect the same from you. Now repeat after me, "I promise on my heritage to devote all of my attention and strength to this game with Cordele,; to exert every effort to defeating our opponents, showing no mercy until the contest is over". All did as directed. Bud, "let's hear it now for the Pioneers, our namesake from our ancestors in this privileged land. Six fifteen at the stadium; if you need wrapping, come earlier; you know the lineup; you subs read your plays this afternoon as it is likely that you will play. If you do I will work you to the bone. One cheer and then fade away to your homes".

Morgan thought, "impressive from the Captain; if it can be done, it will". She got a ride home with some kids and just continued to think on school, the team and Bud. The phone rang shortly and it was Bud, " Morgan, how was the rally?". She, "great, your address was just the right medicine for all of us". Bud, "can we go out after the game? They have a little social planned for after the game; we can stay a few, then fade away; usual for those with dates?" M. "it suits me and I'm hard to please". Bud laughed, "see yah at the gym after the battle".

Morgan got a ride to the stadium; arriving about 7:15 P'*; the game started at 7:45 so she just moved around, greeting friends and soon to be friends. The team warmed up, with Bud right on target with his passes. The left halfback even threw one on the run connecting with the crossing end. About 7:25 they went to the bench as Bud and a guard went out for the coin toss; Cordele won and wanted to receive. The coach gathered his defense, not too large, with two linebackers stong as oxen and 4 defensive backs, quick as deer. A couple of inside linemen anchored the defense. The kicker was rather small; we hoped that he did not have to tackle the receiver. Coach, "they have their speed merchant at receiver; he favors right up the middle as he knows that the sidelines bunch up. Remember he gave us fits last year on kickoffs and punts filling in at halfback the second half. The ends pinch in after our 45; it'll take all of you to hem him up". Bud, "remember what I said this afternoon; hit hard and someone will drop the ball sooner or later".

The ball was over and over and the lightning one had it; he started up the middle but a couple of our backs got him down at their 35. The first play was up the middle behind the left guard, the runner getting 4 hard yards as the linebacker "popped" him. This runner was slow getting up so we knew that he wouldn't get the ball for a while. The fullback tried the right guard, but our man shook off the block and stood the runner up. Would they pass now? Not long to wait as they split the ends out and put a halfback in the slot to the left. The snap was taken but our tackle was chasing him in the backfield; he threw toward the left end, the ball off his fingertips into the waiting hands of the defensive back, who was moving as he caught it, down our right sideline to the goal. The kicker hit it through for a 7-0 lead.

Prosperity kicked off again to the same receiver; he took it straight up the middle to his 40 when a defensive back downed him. They were consistent, trying the middle of the line twice before missing a pass. In punt formation, the center missed the punter and there was a scramble for the ball. Actually, it was Prosperity's ball on Cordele's 37. Bud faked a reverse to a flanker then caught the left end open for 20 yards. The left halfback broke through the line for 10 and it was first and goal. Bud bootlegged around right end for the score, carrying their safety for the last few yards. The extra point made it 14-0. Another kickoff left Cordele on its 35 and they put the ball in the air, completing a short pass. A run got their first down and they tried another pass picked off by Prosperity's left cornerback who was tackled promptly.

Bud went to the runs, first the fullback, then the right halfback, then an option by him keeping the ball. A well oiled machine hammering out the yardage; their defensive backs moved up just before Bud hit the right halfback with one around the 5, an easy TD. The point made a Blackjack, 21-0. Another kickoff for t he 2d quarter; the Coach began to feed in the replacements. They were actually tougher than the 1st team. Two more TDs before the half stretched the score to 35-0.

A short intermission, then back to work; the coach gave Bud a new backfield to work with and he put them to work; the 3rd quarter seeing the score go to 49-0. The bench was emptied as the regulars became fans. It was dullsville as Cordele finally got on the scoreboard with a long pass. 49-7 was the final. The social was in the gym, within walking distance of the stadium so Morgan walked over. The boys came a bit later after showering(needed); all the girls were standing around, sipping punch and talking the smallest conversation possible.

Before long, Bud and the team showed up; they surely looked differently than when in their 'war' togs. He came over to Morgan. "Morg, we were fortunate tonight; Cordele has played better against us". Morgan "Bud, don't you think that the hard work all of you did these past three weeks helped you in this game?". B "you know, you're only 100% right; our training put us in shape to stand in with any team in our conference". M." Now, that's right; the home field doesn't hurt does it? Bud "they say a dog bites harder in his yard and I agree". Both had some punch and sort of slid off by themselves to whisper. Bud "I'll manage to slip out the back door and you may come 'looking' for me". Morgan." roger out, Q back". He moved like a cat, disappearing as discussed; Morgan waited a few then moved to the front of the gym, seeming to be searching for him".

As she went out the front, he drove up with the aqua convertible, sleek as a jaguar; she popped herself in and the couple were on their way. He just drove without saying too much. Morgan's curiosity got the best of her" Bud where are we going?".

Bud. "we can go to the drive in for a sandwich and then ride down to the Flint (River) and just watch the scenery or go to the last movie." Morgan, "sounds good, all of it; I'm starving or almost so the sandwich is first". B. imitating Jackie Gleason, "And away we go". Shortly we were there at 'teen heaven', deciding to eat in the car. The young lady came out, likely one who needed the work; Morgan was always courteous to working girls. They ordered 2 bar-b-cues, french fries and iced tea (the standby). In a flash she brought our food, the sandwich was chipped cue with Georgia vinegar- based sauce, the fries still had the skin on and the tea had frosted the glass. She thought, "Bud thought of everything; this guy is a keeper, if I can land him".

We took our time, he gave our waitress a substantial tip and we departed. He said "the tip was more because she really needs the money". M "Bud I'm glad that you are generous, especially with those who are in need". We chatted as I made up my mind about the river or the movie. I thought that the outside, nature, the moon shining on the water, was the right choice, "Bud how about the Flint?" He smiled "I hoped that you'd say that as I wanted you to have a choice of spots; not my choice always". It was only 15 minutes or less before we reached the landing; the Flint was a long waterway, beginning at Atlanta and winding through middle Georgia, down through SW Georgia. A fairly large river for the area, provided fishing, water skiing, swimming and irrigation when needed.

Bud pulled up on the bank above the water, turned off the car and looked at Morgan, no talk, just a pleasant gaze. Morgan had to speak, "A penny for your thoughts". Bud "I'm sure they are worth more as they are about you". Morgan "it seems that this is our first opportunity to be together and alone. I can get used to it". Bud smiled, "it's growing on me already; who sent you to our town?" M. "it seems as if it was the peanut mill and what I stayed away from at first is now what I need and want". Bud "Morg, you seem more mature than your age would suggest; we fit together, if I can say, as if we'd known each other forever".

Then they just sat there, looking at each other; no gestures or movements; the moon was rising, shining on the water. Morgan, "are you sore from the game?" He said, "not now but in the morning and all tomorrow". They danced around, each with his/her thoughts. "why doesn't he kiss me?" B." she is so lovely; I can't mess her hair, lipstick or anything. Maybe I can get a clue if she wants me to, but how?" An idea popped up in Bud's cranium..." what if I ask her to rub my arm, maybe with a lubricated tissue?". Here he goes, "Morgan I have some medicated tissue -like tissues; could you rub my right arm with one?".

Morgan, smiling, "Bud, you know that I'd like that; maybe take the soreness or some of it, out". Now Bud smiled as he retrieved the tissues from the glove compartment, handing one to her. Since he had on short sleeves, it was easy for her to rub his arm, especially the biceps. She did it nicely, at times, Bud helped her. The closeness was invigorating and actually made the wanting worse. As she finished, he eased the medication from her, still holding her close. She did not move away as he turned her face to his, lightly bussing her on her cherry lips; her lips held his tightly for a vigorous kiss. Then they disengaged; both looking at the other; Bud spoke first, "Wow, I've wanted to do that since we met but I was too timid". Morgan, "true confessions; I wanted you to kiss me but I thought it might be forward; we both came to our senses at the same time".

Bud, "I hate to break this up but we both need to get back to our nests; this night was (is)great and I'll remember it forever. In a few, Bud cranked the car and eased it towards town. When he arrived at her house, he stopped some distance from her door, put up the top and reached for her as she moved towards him. They kissed as only two who really care for each other. Yes, her lipstick was smeared just a bit but the night might conceal the mischief. He eased on up to her door; opened the car, assisted her out and walked her to the door. She had her key so they both said their goodbyes quickly and Bud exited.

Inside, Morgan just smiled and ran over the events of the last 40 minutes; she was his and he was hers. Those facts are accepted. She, a newbie, and him, scion of the Southland were joined; she had really never had a connection like this, just little boys and tiny girls. She took off her makeup, washed her face and put her night clothes on. She was still so hyped up that sleep would come slowly. She mused, "our thoughts are very similar; he cares about others, he's not selfish, he's inquiring, patient and loving".

Sleep did come and she took advantage of it; when she awoke, the house was quiet; she didn't know that her Mother was shopping for groceries. She adjusted quickly, obtaining some coffee already made and making cheese toast. Not long before the cell rang; she prayed that it was Bud. It WAS. One word led to another and so on. Finally, he asked if she was busy this afternoon (Sat) and she replied, NO. Bud said, "can you come for the afternoon and dinner; I'll see that you're home by 9P ". Morgan, Mom's gone but I'm sure that it's OK so lets count on it. What time may I expect you?" Bud, "maybe 3:30P, OK?" All set.

Morgan stayed busy until 2:45 P when she began to get 'ready' for the dinner with Bud's family. She thought about the right outfit to wear, coming to the conclusion that a dress, no hose, flat shoes; no showing of the bodice except just a hint. She shampooed her hair, did her nails AND toenails (open-toed shoes). Mom had returned and approved the date so the green light was on. Her preparation was thorough and when completed, she was a knockout. The dress was new from one of Cordele's dress shops, new not a holdover from the past year. Now for the purse; it must be small, carried in one hand, holding only her compact for touch-up makeup and her house key. It was not always easy for a girl under 5'5" to find a dress the right length as well as the correct mid-size/waist-size. Her Mother was a superb critic of her purchases so they were always perfect. Yes, altering s always an option but right makes the lady.

She watched the clock as it slowly moved to 3:30; looking outside, Morgan viewed the aqua convertible. She opened the door as he knocked, saying, "Mom, Bud's here". We scooted to the car, under way in a jiffy. Again, Bud drove slowly while we talked, more easily now. He had sacked in most of the AM, then went with his Dad to informally appraise a house that the Bank, C and S, was to make a loan on. Bud wasn't trained but his Dad had done this, many times with various banks. A frame house was more difficult to appraise than a stucco or brick dwelling. Anyway, they wrapped it up shortly after Noon, had lunch downtown and came home.

Pulling into the circular driveway, Morgan felt like it was showtime; this little girl had to make an impression on Bud's parents AND she would. He parked in front, and they entered the front entrance. His Mother was moving from the kitchen to the dining room. The table seated 12 persons so I guessed that we would dine at one end. She greeted me; she was about the age of my Mother, well dressed, pleasant and talkative. She took away the nervousness that I felt; the Dad was taking a siesta and the servants had been excused for the evening after preparing the meal. Bud, "Morgan we raise quail, the S. Georgia national bird; the pens are in the far back; may I show them to you?" M. "I'd love it, Bud".

We excused ourselves and walked some distance to the back of the 5 acres; the pens were on legs, to prevent predators from consuming them. Some had small 'biddies' about as big as a thimble with a couple of grown females to watch them. Then there were the pens, screened wire affixed to 2X4s, that held males and females. When the younger ones had grown some; it didn't take long; they would try to plant a 'covey' on land devoid of these wonderful birds. Once this was done, as the covey grew, they would divide to make 2 coveys and so on. This was called the 'Fall Shuffle'.

We walked a bit further to the bantam coops; the small chickens whose eggs and progeny matched their sizes. Just as active as regular chickens BUT reduced in size. Why? We don't know as Bud opined but his desire was to see IF they could or would mix with the normal sized poultry. The only other comparable bird in this area, per Bud, was the guinea fowl, always loose, scavenging for a worm or insect. They were reckless, always crossing the road just before a vehicle. The saying was 'you can't run over a guinea' BUT I'm not so sure.'

The clock was running towards 6P and dinner was at 6: 30 without fail. Country folks set their meals by their stomachs, at least Dad's stomach for dinner. This was his meal with the family and ALL had better be there UNLESS they were quail hunting or out of the country. The meals were usually varied with always tomatoes (in season), pepper sauce, a meat, vegetable and a salad. The dessert was optional for all except Dad. He savored the sweets, homemade in a churn in 9 months of the year with a pie the other three.

Bud and Morgan just ambled along towards the house, entering the back, using the half bath to 'wash up', even if the ladies didn't need it. Morgan sprinkled her hands as Bud soaped his thoroughly. Why do men's hands get so dirty, thought Morgan? She, "Bud, don't take off the skin" as he rubbed and rubbed. Bud," you know that stadium mud doesn't give up easily". She laughed as everything between them was new and exciting. In the dining room, Mrs. Carter said softly, "Morgan, if it's Ok, you may sit first on the right side, next to Dad at the end, Bud can sit on his left and I'll sit on Morgan's right". Mr. Carter, "now that Rose has designated our places, Bud will say the grace". Bud, "our Father......all our blessings......help us to assist others who are not so fortunate........Amen". Rose, "Bud we're used to it but it's always comforting". Mr.Carter sat and so did we. The food looked so delicious to Morgan, that within her mind, she was already 'chowing down'. The dishes passed the ham, potato salad, tomatoes and French bread. The pear salad with a dab of mayo was adjacent to all plates.

Mr. Carter, "Morgan, they tell me that you just moved from Ashburn, another peanut town?" M, "yessir, I was born there on a frosty December morning in 1985; my sister at Mercer is 7 years older". Mr. Carter "what do you think of our little paradise?". M "my first week is so busy but my impressions are that Ashburn is in the rear-view mirror". Mr. Carter and Rose laughed at the comparison. Bud, "Morgan is already in with her classmates and some of mine; it's like she has been forever". Rose, "Morgan, it is busy times when one uproots from a known place to an unknown location but your transition sets a new record". M. "thank you both for your hospitality to me; Bud has been a lifesaver". Mr. C, "I'll bet that's true". They all laughed, then began the meal. Afterwards, Mr. Carter had his coffee with his vanilla ice cream; all but Mrs. Carter tried the ice cream, avowing that it was the best ever.

We all sat on the screened porch afterwards reviewing the football game with Cordele.

Bud said" I didn't miss that large tackle and fast defensive end from last year; someone said that the tackle got a scholarship to UGA this year; my body feels better with him in Athens". They laughed. Mr. Carter "the Coach has you guys ready to play; you all seemed as fresh as a daisy the whole game, even if you were on the field almost 2/3 of the time". Bud "our defense was all over them, those quick defensive backs of ours can ruin our opponents". They agreed that the team showed UP and OUT, whipping one of their usual tough opponents.

After some time, Mom and Dad (the Carters) slipped away for their private times; Morgan and Bud, like two youngsters, just looked at each other and smiled. They had some time before she had to leave so they sat together in the porch swing, swinging slowly, holding hands to insure that neither strayed too far from the other. The smell of Confederate Jasmine was in the air, giving it a pleasant nectar, bringing back memories of childhood with their scents from generations.

Bud leaned over, touching her lips lightly with his own; she responded by pulling him closer for a real welcome. He exhaled, then inhaled the fragrance of a vibrant, alive and healthy young woman. Her scent was so overwhelming, a combination of youth, cleanliness and passion. Bud caught his breath, barely uttering "Morgan, can we leave now?" She said, "as you wish, do we go somewhere before home?" B "I want to". M "Me too".

Leaving the house. Morgan was so proud of Bud's family; they are 'old' Georgia, going back to when the frontiers of Georgia were just being settled, by the Scotch and the English. The Cherokees, in North Georgia, were in the 1840s, forced by the Federal Government to trek to Oklahoma, in a bitter resolution of the so-called Cherokee 'problem', which was actually a 'white man's' issue.

Bud, driving slowly, was heading away from Morgan's home; she alerted looking at him intensely, he said, "I always wanted to see the Coliseum empty with no lights on". Morgan giggled, "you goose, why didn't you say so?". B "you are too kind ". He pulled to a stop in the shadow of the stadium, switched off, turning to her as she slid towards her. She was near Bud as he circled his right arm around her right shoulder; she knew the direction of this and desired it. She graciously lifted her face towards his, lips touching, binding, emitting the scent of Spearmint, every Swain's salvation. Deeply within her psyche, Morgan felt her head spinning as she continued the kiss. Finally, they parted, both exhaling, a bit dizzy over the extended buss. The look that passed between them was one of affection and faith. Bud did not remove his arm from Morgan; she looked a natural in his loose embrace.

He cranked, driving slowly towards Morgan's home, both with their own thoughts and emotions, quietly enjoying these. Morgan "Bud, did you want to leave the stadium?" He looked at her with a quizzical look, "what do you think?". She smiled, "the right answer". Just short of the light rays from her front door light, he pulled over, reached over and gently slid her over to him. This kiss was full of desire, respect and care for her; she closed her eyes, opened her lips slightly to receive him AND the bargain of affection was instilled in both.

As Bud left her front door, Morgan just sunk in a chair to regain her composure; this date was like cement; as it dries it becomes permanent. She knew now that they are a match, a great one AND her maturity was coming rapidly. She showered, taking off her makeup; putting the medication on her face and then sinking into her bed. Leaving her bed lamp on as she could not sleep; Morgan just lay there, looking at the ceiling, then started recording events in her diary. This day was too important to not write down; wow, was her life flying by?" After some time, her eyelids felt gritty and she knew that sleep was with her. Moreover, she planned to go to Sunday School at the First Baptist and, likely, stay for the Sermon. Maybe, she and Bud could start going together to Church?

Waking Sunday Morning at what time? she jumped out of bed, laid out her best garment, then, dressed, grabbed a cup of coffee and asked her Dad to drive her to Church. Morgan "I can't stand not having a drivers' license; let December arrive very soon". She arrived at the Church, needing to inquire where her age group met. Rushing to the room, entering; she saw many schoolmates, who greeted her. The teacher was giving a lesson as she signed in the class. Morgan caught the final 30 minutes of the New Testament, Mark, an important recording of the Gospels.

Enjoying the lesson, Morgan lingered a minute or so to speak to her schoolmates. Then all of them went into the church before all the back seats were taken. They sat together as the ceremony began with singing and the reading of biblical writings. Then to the sermon by Dr. Clark, longtime minister of the First Baptist. He had overseen the growth of this church for 10 years and the construction of this building. The Baptists had no policy of rotation of its ministers as long as the congregation supported him. He started very slowly, building up to more volume, maybe to wake up the snoozers. His delivery was good and he ended with an important point. Morgan liked it and as they exited, she was asked to ride with one f the girls.

At home, she ate lightly, a sandwich, milk and a small piece of cake. Then she went to her room to study OR just think. She really needed both. Morgan's head was spinning with good thoughts about Mr. Bud, her first real boyfriend. So many thoughts raced through her head like 'visions of sugarplums danced through her head' the old fairy tale. Did it really happen as she imagined? Was she the luckiest girl in Worth County or maybe the whole state?

She had to get down to studying or she could wind up staying after school to study. Not good, Girl. This Trig was a bear so she needed to see who was good at it AND study with her. Bud was too far ahead to help her out so she was flying on one wing. She toyed all afternoon but found herself writing 'Bud Carter' over and over in her composition.

Bud called about a ride out, just to break the monotony; Morgan was game so she put on shorts and a Tee and met him at the door. He looked like Adonis from Greek Mythology, tall, tanned, eyes sparkling, Mr. Neat, the whole salami. Morgan didn't want to reveal her feelings too early BUT might not be able to conceal these desires. He was always upbeat and his good nature was catching. They just rode in the country, sticking to the paved (hard) roads, enjoying the scenery. Bud said "I want to show you something". He turned off on a dirt road, driving slowly until he came to a creek; it was sparkling, clean, pristine with space for two cars on its bank. We sat for a spell and talked for bit as he reached to help me over to him, no resistance from me. The kiss was sweet, neat and welcome as she joined in the mild petting of that day. They both needed some release from day to day activities. This was perfect. For 15 minutes, her tantalizing mouth engulfed Bud's with some time out for catching their breaths; she began to repair her makeup as Bud turned the car to exit the 'hideaway'. Both knew that they needed to go.

Bud dropped her off, Morgan "you don't have to go the door every time, when we have a casual outing" He, "thanks, it does give us a few seconds more BUT you know how I respect you?" M."I know much more than that about you". Bud smiled "and I about you". She went to the house as Bud drove off; would he call tonight? Maybe or Yes. Morgan went back to her studies so as to meet Monday AM with some preparation. She did keep the radio on with soft rock or listening music, the kind that puts one to sleep.

She almost forgot that she needed to do her nails and toenails; to omit these could be a blot on her character. With open-toed shoes, any failure was immediately noticed; she had to be on her toes as the new girl on the block.

CHAPTER III:
A ROUTINE

Beginning her 2d week of school, it seemed to Morgan that she'd been there maybe 6 months; the routine was what it was; thank providence for Bud, the cheerleader for us all. His personality was so pleasant that no one ever got into a disagreement with him. How great. Morgan was pleasant to everyone but she could stand her ground when she felt that she was right. Of course, females rarely battle in public, preferring to 'snipe' at the opponent and lay traps for her to embarrass her before the gang or the audience. It wasn't long before she was accepted as just one of the ladies. The ice was broken without her falling in.

Bud was picking her up in the AM for school but football practice spoiled the PM ride. She could ride with anyone going her way but It was always having to check before the last bell rang. Talk about Bud's quail, they couldn't be any faster than these students getting out of the building. All types of hotrods filled the parking lots; converted Chevrolets and Fords, 57 Chevrolets, 58 Fords (police specials); all adapted for some purpose, I. e. looks, speed, space comfort. These farm boys who worked on tractors, could tear down an engine almost before the girls could solve a trig problem. A few looked as if they were left over from the Vietnam war. But they moved these students twice a day for 9 months. The team for Prosperity practiced all week on pass defense; dropping the end or linebacker from the likely side of the pass, to bolster the secondary.

It's difficult to teach a 'back' how to play defense against an experienced attack. All were concerned about the quarterback for Perry who had set some records this year. Now, the downside was that they lost 4 games, each by less than 7 points. BUT they could put points on the board NOW and THEN. A couple of their scores were 35-31 v Tift County; 24-27 Dooly County and 21-26 Warner Robins, from a higher division. It was known that they could score and Prosperity could stop some scoring; was this the unstoppable force against the immovable force?

The 'boys' left for Perry on Saturday at 5P, two busses this time for the cheerleaders and flag girls. The coach was going all out to give the guys all support possible. A motorcade was leaving at 5:35P with most fans decking their vehicles (including trucks and jalopies) with the green/yellow school colors, pom poms and country attachments.

Morgan went with a friend, who had no drivers' license either; another Father-Daughter deal ,but they got to Perry, arriving around 7P. Parking was awful but her Dad slid it in an open space that was somehow missed. Out of the car in a flash, Dad in the ticket line as they looked through the wire at the warm-ups. Inside, they saw the sparsely filled stands for the visitors. However, this changed over 30 minutes to give Prosperity respectability.

No lights for now, daylight was still with Perry. Bud and the rest were passing the football; just light stuff, giving the receivers some loosening up. If Perry passed, how good were they against the pass. Bud was ready for an air show and so were the receivers. He had not needed to throw much this year but this game was different. Bud was hitting them on the run, maybe a bit too hard, but they caught most. Maybe he could lighten up a little in the game; but one must remember that a lightly thrown football was anybody's prize.

The cheerleaders, et al were on the sidelines; the band marched into the stands. As they cranked up, the cheerleaders began to do flips and all types of gymnastics; the crowd loved it. The boys came to the sideline for extra taping and their words from the Coach and Bud. Coach "you've all worked hard this year; you can be proud of this. I'm asking for one more effort from you. We haven't faced a passer like their guy; he has taken apart most of his opponents. Our defensive backs have to be alert and quick; be careful about tackling a couple of their receivers, they are shifty and can shake off a mild tackle. If needed, Bud will open it up in the second half. Go get 'em".

Bud, " I don't need to say much; we've seen some tough games in the past. I want to start with Moose' from Fullback in the first quarter, running behind the center and guards. If they move a linebacker in, we'll counter with the opposite tackle. I'll run him until they catch on; then it's our left halfback. If they gang up on him, I'll shift to the double reverse, with the left halfback taking my handoff heading to right, handing to the right halfback going left. This might slow down their rapid reaction to our crossbucks. Give me all that you have.

The coin toss was won by Prosperity, whose deep man it back to the 40. Bud and crew came on, the fullback plunging up the middle for 8. Bud fed him the ball for; first down, then another 5, 6 more for a first. Bud tried a bootleg around the right end for 6 yards; then the double reverse, first to the right handing off to the right halfback for an open scamper around for 18 yards to their 16. Back to the fullback, 4 plunges over the goal. The Pat was good.

Perry got the ball deep as one of their speedsters ran it to their 35. We got a look at the quarterback as he held his huddle. They came out with a back split to their left as we dropped the right end back 5-6 yards. Both their right end an d flanker went straight for ten yards, the flanker going towards the sideline; the pass hit him as our end tackled him. First down, a play into the middle, a short pass to the left end for 6, 3rd and 2. He sneaked for 3, another first. A pass over the middle for 11 yards. Time out Prosperity; a shift of the middle linebacker to the defensive backfield, just 12 yards back for him.

A run by Perry was stuffed, a halfback pass was broken up; they went for their right sideline, overshooting the receiver. A punt to our 15 that the back caught on the fly, hot-footing it to the 40. Bud and the Fullback took over with 5 straight runs, 2 Firsts; catch their breaths, then a trap play on their right tackle, springing the left HB for 12. A quick pitch to the right HB got 7, then the FB got the 1st down. The left end crossed the middle, took the bullet and faked their left corner-back; just easing in for the score. 14-0

Another kickoff where the receiver almost got loose, being downed near midfield. A pass to their right end got them 12 as he went OOB. Another pass to a back over the middle gathered 9; a plunge over guard got 2 for a first. A reverse pass caught another back on the 15; he went in untouched. Pat for 14-7. Bud and crew got the kickoff driving it steadily downfield, stalling on the 6yard line. The field goal made it 17-7. The half ended.

In the second half, Perry got the ball, passing almost every down. They caught a cornerback asleep, hit a fast end for 6. Now with the Pat 17-14. They seemed tougher or was it that we weren't at our best. Bud spoke before the kickoff "you know now that we are in a game; give me your full attention. We have found that we can run so let's do it. The kickoff sailed to the ten, being fielded by one of the fasted backs on the team. He flew down the middle, got a block or two, then gutted it down to the Perry 40. The Fullback for 4 plunges, 5, 4, 3, 7, the halfback for 4; first down again, A double reverse to the left, Bud to the left HB, he handed to the right halfback, the fullback leading him to the Perry 10.

The fullback for 3 runs over the goal. Pat, 24-14. The rest of the 3rd quarter was devoted to a series of mishaps. In the 4th, Perry was at midfield; still hammering Prosperity with passes, mostly short. The defensive backs were better but the receivers were fast and shifty. It was a dogfight until there was only 1:15 left on the clock. Their quarterback went to the air; a few were knocked down but he gained ground. The clock was running, with 20 seconds left when he found a man open, hitting him to the 1yard line. A plunge got the TD; the pat made it 24-21 with 3 seconds left. The onside kick hit our lineman who fell on it. Game over

It was difficult to tell who was more tired, the fans or the team. All needed a rest so back to Worth County. No dates tonight.

The trip back home was a proud one but not a whole lot of talking.

CHAPTER IV: THE TWISTS OF FATE

All got home late, showered and turned in. Morgan slept in that morning, still tired from the travel and excitement. She studied all day, talking to Bud twice.

The week coming was exciting as the football players received their jackets, with the large P and the golden football as well as the stripes, 1 for each year of playing. Bu*d sought Morgan as she looked for him. He held out the jacket to her; she donned it* even though it looked quite large. Morgan would have worn it regardless. School was still school, but what else would Morgan do?

Morgan and Bud did study together, usually at her house; Bud was cruising on his studies as she had some difficulty with Trig and Contemporary Writing, both hard cases for a Freshwoman. Trig could wrap a very good student somewhat similar to writing Chinese without prior study. They both knew that this had to be done so they got on it. It wasn't always easy to keep their minds on studies, as her perfume was permeating his senses. A knockout of a lady, with the appropriate graces, and social intuition sitting next to her boyfriend, who is full blooded and ready, can interfere with proper studying.

Prosperity lost the last playoff to Gainesville in Gainesville 21-17; some did not go because of the distance. A great season to be topped off by the Harvest Dance in the gym; the Frosh and Sophomores would decorate the gym and the guys would drive them out to gather the moss and plants for the backdrop. There were good reasons for substituting wild plant for a once a year dance; money was not plentiful despite the fine crops. By the time, the farmer paid his fertilizer, seed, gasoline and repair bills, not counting his personal responsibilities, he was no longer flush. As the price of crops and groceries went up, so did other costs.

The basketball games had begun, Tuesday and Friday nights, so to keep from being bored, Bud, Morgan and a flock of other students, formed the cheering section. A few of the FB players played basketball and even baseball in the Spring. The schools that had no football teams got an early start on basketball, showing up quickly with good teams.

This continued until March when it slowed and baseball began. A good number of Prosperity football team members also played baseball, including Bud. In the winter, at various times, a farm family would have a barn dance to remind us of long gone times. They were great, drinking cider, eating Brats and shelling parched peanuts. Thank goodness that all customs aren't going away.

Bud and Morgan usually went, excusing themselves early to have some private time. In the Winter, the car was too cold unless it was running so sitting in it talking or playing was not an option. So, what was? This was an issue until someone came up with the idea of a bus ride before the 'dance'. They put a few bales of hay in the bus so they could pretend. This way, all could have some privacy under the blanket outside the prying eyes of some chaperones. No all viewed this as did

Bud and his friends. Morgan thought it was great even with a blanket, for the cold of course.

To drive away the boredom, a number of students came up with super ideas to get together with or without dates AND without spending any great amount of money.

Morgan still had conversations with her parents, unlike some who were 'too busy'. They usually ate dinner together, but breakfast was hectic and lunch was at school. Of course, the lunch was for talking and getting the news on all the students. With the classes backed up on one another, there was no other time to 'just talk'. The physical education was great if we didn't have some exercise to learn. We jabbered at that, greatly enlightening us on the social scene, Morgan thought. What about Morgan's classmates? They were cut from the same cloth; why not know who went with whom and who had broken up and who had made up.

Even with all the social life, the Winter was still the Winter but Spring was on the way. The trees were budding and most plants were beginning to 'put out'. The gardens were being planted according to The Farmers' Almanac, good enough for Dad, good enough for son. In early April, the school had a 'Beauty and Talent Contest'; only 18 girls entered as many could not afford the dress required OR did not have a talent to display. The contest was entered by girls from all four grades. Quite a group of ladies, most with commendable talents. It was clear from the beginning that Morgan had the looks; did she have a talent to display? She had piano lessons in grade school and had danced for a while. Could she perform a dance by solo? She bore down on a talent, finally settling on a voice presentation. The song, "Battle Hymn of the Republic" was perfect for this colleen.

The night arrived and many performed very well; Morgan held her own with the song as her beauty and charm won the night. She would be the entrant for the Macon beauty contest ten days later. She was prepared to face beauties from the whole state. Her Mother went with her to Macon although she had her driver's license since last December. There was heavy competition from the contestants, however, she made the final 5, where all were evaluated by questioning, talent and looks. After some time; each being questioned, the Judges found Morgan to be number one. She received $500 plus publicity and a trophy two feet high.

School was concluding and she needed a job so she pressed her father for anything to make some money; and to stay busy in the daytime. Her Dad was looking but, nothing so far. She checked with the Principal and he said that grades 5-6-7 were looking for a tutor for summer school; these students had not met all the requirements. The times would be 9-11, 5 days a week for 5 weeks; there would be another session for others and any of these who failed to pass their assigned period. She would teach American history and English and earn 60% of a teacher's salary. Wow.

In the summer things were humming along; she was employed and so was Bud, at the bank, doing anything that others wouldn't do. Seeing Bud nightly and working daily kept any boredom away. It was mid August, football practice was beginning and, for Morgan, it was time for her school wardrobe. Another trip to Cordele was in order.

School started around Labor Day and football started that Friday. The team missed some of the Seniors departed; trying to fill the gaps with raw recruits or others who had little experience. It was not to be a great year, even though the young squad played their hearts out. Bud was demoralized but failed to show it. Morgan did her best to keep his spirits up.

Football came and went, the team was 6-4, not great but with outstanding determination. Bud was still his usual gritty player but the support was lacking. Bud thought, and he was right, that a school needed at least 40-43 players IF the team was to sustain itself with experience year after year. Prosperity had only 28 or so, not nearly enough to provide trained replacements.

Things were good with our two, they were in love and their physical attractions were mutual. He was honorable and she was pristine BUT the combination was bound to go further, seeking release from the stress. Christmas came with the usual barn dance, syrup candy making and barn fires.

On to the end of March for the Beauty Contest; should Morgan enter this contest or perhaps enter a larger one in Savannah or Atlanta? She could go back to Macon; she had been invited. Macon, it was and another trophy was won. Very unusual for any girl to win back to back first place awards.

It was strange with Bud gone to UGA, almost like a deserted town as seen in the movies in the West. He wanted to keep up the football and UGA had a history of great Quarterbacks. But would he play Quarterback? He would play where needed. He and Morgan talked almost nightly; this assisted both in avoiding a painful boredom. Morgan wondered about her future; could she remain home for two years? Doubtful. She was loyal but this separation tested both. In many ways, she regretted not having a physical relationship with Bud; she now wanted one more than ever but, would she ever have it?

She struggled through to Christmas break; Bud was coming for twelve days. She had saved her virginity this long but it wouldn't last much longer. It was overrated in Morgan's estimation. Love is love is love. Morgan mused 'there is only one youthful period for each; if we fail to use it, then the moment is lost forever'.

Bud would be back on Dec 14; we had to go out that night, says Morgan. The days crept by, vacation wasn't so great, thought Morgan. Then it arrived, Bud was back at his house but with Morgan on the phone. He knew that he had to divide his time so the afternoon was for his Dad and Mom; the evenings from 6P on were solely for Morgan.

He picked her up in the Toyota Camry, given to him when he left for UGA. It was just a bit smaller than the Convertible, but was a beauty. It was beige with the same interior. Bud asked" where do you want to go?" Morgan "to our special brook". He headed in that direction; as the time had changed, 6P was approaching darkness. Bud pulled in and turned the car around to face towards the exit. Then he reached for her; Morgan was there swiftly. They kissed and again, both saying" I really missed you ". They kissed and talked; gradually Bud discovered the buttons, on the left side of her blouse; he began at the top, working down the row. Morgan was not surprised at this; in fact, welcomed it. She removed her blouse displaying her full brassiere.

Bud was mesmerized by this sight; it was different from a packed sweater. Slowly he reached behind her, unhooking the garment. When it loosened, both breasts emerged with pink tips on each. What now, she thought? Bud leaned over, kissing each nipple, each standing erect. This continued with Bud very involved; his midsection brushed against her; his manhood had risen and she knew it. He rubbed against Morgan, as their breaths came faster. His hand massaged her leg as it went up to her private area. She caught her breath as Bud ran his finger lingo of that day stated. Then Bud 'took' her and she surrendered. On the way back to town, the silence was overwhelming. Talk could come later. They stopped for a snack, eating in the car. The talk came slowly, as molasses pouring from a frozen jug.

They didn't talk about what just happened, 'the thing' as some related to it or a dozen other unusual sayings. They made small talk after the drive-in, each with his/her own thoughts; but the affection was there and the respect. Sometime later he took her home, giving her a super kiss before she went inside. She heard the phone ring; it was her sister, Marsha, from Macon. Morgan" what's wrong?" Marsha "nothing, I'm just enjoying the holiday season and Wayne and I want to come down for a night". Morgan had met Wayne once; he was graduating from

Medical School and going on for his residency in internal medicine. Her Mother was still up so she asked when it would be convenient for Marsha and Wayne to come down. Her Mother replied "either the 23rd or the 26th". Marsha "the 23rd is fine". It's settled. Marsha and Morgan chatted a few minutes even though there was a 7 year difference in their ages. Morgan only said that Bud was home from UGA as Marsha extolled the virtues of her Wayne. Morgan thought 'he's a cold fish but if that's the menu at Mercer, so be it'. Her Mother was thinking of the sleeping arrangements as they had 3 beds only plus a couch/sleeper. Morgan "she can sleep with me or he can take the sleeper, might loosen him up a bit".

Morgan terminated the call as both needed to go to bed. Why is it that we say 'go to bed' rather than 'go to sleep' thought Morgan? Is it that we are so inquisitive about the smallest?

Time flew during December as Bud and Morgan fed on each other; two young people coming into adulthood, secure, enthusiastic and focused. They were like most their ages, enjoying the pleasures of youth, combining them with some of the pleasures of adults. Bud found his way to the drugstore for the 'golden coins' that protected both of them. Morgan knew about them but had not been close to such items; she felt very good that Bud 'looked after her', not gambling with their futures. Morgan seemed a bit more mature, possibly from the change to her body.

The 23rd came; Marsha and Wayne drove up around 10A or so; the family went out to greet them. Wayne was his usual highbrow self as Marsha was her usual gushy, cheerful, pleasant college Senior. All talked some; then Mother suggested that they bring the luggage (overnight bags) into the house. Mother showed Wayne his room, informing Marsha that she would sleep with Morgan. Marsha "I haven't done that since high school but I'll enjoy it". Morgan "and I". Lunch was served shortly; it was unusual to have more than 3 at the table. We ate while talking constantly; Marsha couldn't believe that Morgan was a young adult, beautiful, charming, intelligent and composed. The sisters batted the words back and forth as the others listened in awe.

Shortly Bud arrived with his smile and handsome look; greeting Marsha and Wayne with enthusiasm; he had that trait of entrancing almost anyone. We all sat in the living room, watching a Pro football game. Marsha inquired "Bud, what's your status at UGA with football?" Bud "I was redshirted this year; we had 3 other quarterbacks so Coach felt that he needed me to wait a year. I might not play quarterback at all; they're talking about defensive end and I don't mind ". Wayne sat there like a toad, completely lost in the talk of sports. He and Marsha were as far apart as the points of a 180 -degree angle. But it was what it was. Was it his prospects or something deeper? Anyway, he was probably destined to be in the family sooner than later.

Since they had to go back on the 24th, Morgan suggested that they exchange gifts on the night of the 23rd. They gave Morgan's Mother and Dad a double electric blanket, Morgan a sweater and Bud a jacket. All of the family gave Marsha a long coat and Wayne a valet. After everyone hooting and hollering about the presents, Dad whipped up some egg nogg, not heavy on the nogg. After a few words around the fire, Bud said he had to run to the drugstore, asking Morgan to go with him. She agreed. They departed not for the Pharmacy but for their 'hideaway', a place that would always be in her heart. The motor had barely stopped when Bud grabbed her, holding her gently as they kissed. The kisses revved up Bud and likely, Morgan. He opened her blouse as she unhooked the bra. Again, he muzzled both of her breasts; she shivered for a few seconds before kissing him thoroughly. He was on top of her and she felt his erection. She unzipped his trousers freeing his instrument; her skirt was up to her waist as Bud removed her panties, absorbing a condom. He then inserted it into her as she moaned. It wasn't long before they left to return to her house. All were in their rooms, Marsha in Morgan's, as she entered the house.

Marsha was awake, saying "you're pretty tight with him, aren't you?" Morgan " he's my love, I'd do anything for him". "Well, be careful; you know the ropes, don't you?". Morgan "I hope so". She was tired, dressing for bed promptly. She was so filled with joy and hope that she lay there for a time to calm down.

In the AM, after breakfast, Bud was coming over for the traditional opening of the Yuletide gifts. The two events occurred as Bud rapped on the door. The presents brought by Marsha and ours to them were under the tree, with names affixed. Bud was the mover of these to our guests first; a cashmere sweater to Marsha and a small office micro lens to Wayne; then a double electric blanket to the parents, a travel bag to Morgan and a globe for Bud. After they oohed, aahed and exclaimed, the conversations began without too much output from Wayne. After enough Morgan gave Bud his cue "Bud, don't you have to go the pharmacy?" Bud "yes, I need to go this morning, may I go now?" M "I'll go with you". They scooted out before anyone could say "Jack Daniels". Riding there, Morgan "Bud, what if the employees see me in the car?" Bud "they might guess that the things are for you". M "that's what I'm getting at". Bud," I'm dropping you off on the corner for 5 minutes while I purchase the things; why can't condoms come out of the closet and they quit implying that they cause cancer?" Morgan laughed "actually it could be almost as bad for a scholarship athlete to be rolling a baby carriage at practice". Bud laughed as he let her out on the corner. In 5 he was back with his 'golden coins' put together in 2 pieces.

Off they went to the magic creek, even if it was still in the AM. Morgan asked "is it a sin to fool around in the daylight?". Bud, "I don't see why when everything is clearer". Morgan laughed as she kissed him; in a flash her breasts were uncovered and Bud was exploring them, one at a time, with his tongue. We don't know precisely how Morgan felt about this but she seemed to enjoy anything that Bud did. They were working towards the same goal as she undid her skirt, displaying a very dark inside of her panties. The rest went according to plan, with Bud inside her and both making unusual noises. She put on her face as Bud walked to the creek to wash his hands, Then, back to the house to be with the visitors.

When they entered the house, Marsha "did you have to go to the Cordele Pharmacy?". Morgan almost choked but recovered "they were out so we tried the convenience store". Marsha rolled her eyes; Wayne was comatose. The conversation shifted to their departure, decided to be after lunch. The Mother was preparing sandwiches, soup and iced tea, sweetened of course. Actually, the conversation was thinning; Marsha being 7 years older than Morgan was a gap in interests. There was little to discuss about former friends; Marsha's were graduating or already had, moving all over the globe. Marsha didn't need to hear about the Frosh class of Prosperity and Morgan wasn't giving a peep about 'the creek'.

Morgan was glad that she didn't have a best friend here AS she might be pressured to reveal all the 'creek' activities. God forbid. She knew that Bud was a private person, not one to reveal the deepest secrets. Not even to his teammates, she was confidant.

The lunch was over and Marsha/Wayne were in their car, preparing to leave. The last goodbyes were said and they sped off. Morgan "Bud, what did you think of Wayne?" B "who's Wayne?" Everyone laughed, including Dad. They needed to go to Bud's house so Morgan suggested that. Arriving at the circular drive, Bud parked. Both entered this wonderful house, walking by the family room, the most exquisite Christmas tree was seen. Decked with blue lights and some white ornaments, it looked like a long-ago tree, when people had time to really enjoy the Holiday season. Morgan praised the tree to Bud's Mother, who had decorated it by herself; many prominent families hired someone to prepare their tree but not her. They all had a nice conservation knowing that Bud had to return the day after Christmas to UGA (Univ of Georgia).

Later that afternoon, a few of Bud's high school mates had a dance at a motel in town. No drinking allowed but a few brought a flask, just to liven up themselves. No D Jay, just records but some oldies by the Platters, The Great Pretender, Twilight Time and a few by the Fat Man, Mr. Domino, Blueberry Hill, Good Golly Miss Molly and more, Bud liked the Platters for their smooth delivery and Morgan liked Fats. They both enjoyed it as Morgan tried to teach Bud about Shag, invented in South Carolina who knows when?

Wouldn't you know, someone looked for Bud and her around 9P but no success. They had left through the back door while the others were distracted. Bud knew the routine and the route; only 2 nights left for him with her. No one was in their spot as he turned off the car. Morgan "are we going to do this again?" Bud "unless you know something that is more fun?" Morgan had to agree, 'nothing got them closer than 'it'. They kissed and she felt his manhood, strong and vigorous, as he took her blouse and bra off. The twins stood up erect with their pink noses, Bud tasting of each. Then down to the serious work; she kept her skirt on as Bud removed her panties. One of the golden coins was unwrapped, and then the entry. Morgan caught her breath as this happened then settled into the rhythm.

CHAPTER V:
THE PAIN OF GOODBYES

After dropping her at home, Bud went to his home to plan in his mind the next 36 hours in Prosperity. He knew that 26 Dec was a red letter that all dreaded with intensity. But it must come as the sun arises. On Christmas morning he would be home till after lunch; then to Morgan's for presents; the afternoon was for us; then evening for my house. Sounded good but would it work? Time would tell.

Sleeping a bit late on Christmas, he arose to go into the family room. His parents were there drinking chocolate (hot). He had a cup as he viewed the tree. His presents for his parents were under the tree w/o tags; an electric raiser and a makeup mirror. He asked them not to get him anything but you know how that it? He received a nice stereo and a new cell phone. After breakfast, he went to Morgan's; she was sitting on the sun porch, the sun shining between the pecan trees. He sat with her as she just looked at the scenery, enjoying the wonder of Prosperity. In a short while, she arose, asking Bud just to drive her around to see the decorations; she just got her license but did not have her own car. Her dad had said that "Morgan, we'll do that in the New Year". It would be nice to drive to school and home as well as the basketball games during the week. Bud "let's go and look at the houses and stores". So, they did, seeing all that the town had to show. They just rode through Worth County, marveling at the bare fields. They weren't terribly bare as the farmers had learned to leave the plant residue on the ground to prevent erosion from the Winter rains. Then when they 'broke ground' in late March, the residue could be plowed up, enriching the soil. Another method that was used was to plant bushes thickly around the fields to halt the soil runoffs. New cars were in abundance in the countryside as the bumper crops of peanuts and cotton had let the farmers upgrade their vehicles. Bud took Morgan home to be with parents on Christmas Eve as he went home also. He told Morgan that he'd pick her up at 9A on the 26th. And he was as good as his word, opening the door promptly at 9.

They started driving and she said "Can we see the creek one more time before you go?" Bud nodded, conscious of his impending departure. As he stopped, Morgan moved to him, eager to please him before his solemn trek. He was overcome with passion, taking off her clothing easily, kissing her body at each step. Finally, she lay on her back on the rear seat as Bud cranked the engine, providing warmth that might not be required. He was in the back seat, warming her with his hands as she squirmed around, eager for the next steps. Bud obliged but mindful of the risks, he used the condom. The final insertion was received by Morgan with anticipation. Time stood still as two youngsters displayed their love in the most dramatic fashion. As they drove back to town, no great exchange of words but looks and touching were the methods of communication. He drove her home, kissing her as he left her at the door. He couldn't speak.

Bud left after lunch driving to Athens to the athletic dorm. They wouldn't have practice for several days but would do some chalk boarding on a few new plays. Of course, scheduling classes, obtaining books and other chores kept him busy; he did call Morgan every night; not knowing if this is good or bad but he just had to hear her voice.

Somehow this week was past and a new Quarter meant a new look, Bud hoped. He was taking Algebra, Biology and English Literature, no easy courses. He was not a bad student but for a guy from a very small high school, things can get rough. As classes started, he loosened up, making friends and becoming a real Bulldog. One girl sat next to him in the Lit course, nice looking, well dressed and congenial. They just started talking and Bud shared that this course was difficult for him. She, April, from Augusta, said "Bud, we can study together if you want; the women's dorm has a couple of study rooms where boys are received. "How about tonight about 7P?" she inquired.

Bud was for it so he went that evening to her dorm. They had the room to themselves so the tutoring went well. Bud, for the first time, began to understand the poems, sonnets and odes. He couldn't compose any yet but was able to read and interpret fairly well. April was impressed and said so. Bud beamed as she spoke. They worked till 9:30 when they called it a night; he had to be in by 10:00P. He then called Morgan, forgetting to mention the studying with April. Why, he thought, can't we trust each other? Hmm. For Bud it was not that simple, he was not fickle but when one was accustomed to being around a lovely lady, to be solo was miserable. Besides, there was nothing between she and Bud. Really?

Bud called Morgan each night after his tutoring in English Lit; this did make it difficult to be straight with her but what could he do? April was helping him to overcome his natural reluctance to romantic sonnets composed during Shakespeare's era. She made it so easy to understand and was a superb teacher. This continued; they talked but she never mentioned a boyfriend. Time passed; Bud was faithful to Morgan, only greeting girls; he did tell April about Morgan in the 11th grade. April thought that this was swell but realized the dangers of a long term relationship. She never spoke of her concerns to Bud but began to have some feelings for him, not sure exactly what they were. One night in February, they were studying and Bud's elbow came into contact with her breast; she just smiled as Bud stammered. April "Bud, if anyone was to touch my breast, I prefer you". Bud, "April you know that it was an accident". April "Yes but I liked it". Wow. What does Bud do now? He thought 'I like her, she likes me so, why not?' They agreed that 2 nights a week they'd be social and the other 3 study as now.

Morgan was no dummy; the vagueness of Bud at times was disturbing but how does she get to the root of it? Root has several meanings and Morgan used them all. February sped by and Bud began his dating. There was a cinema on campus and cards (bridge or hearts) to be played anytime. April played bridge so she taught Bud, not an easy task. They paired up with another jock and his girl to do a variety of things. Still no intimacy between them as both were 'playing it cool'. One night Bud and April went to the drive-in movie, one of the very few left, enticing couples who couldn't afford a motel. Bud was sitting as April slid over, bussing him on his lips; then her hand sought another 'root' perhaps more rigid than the ones in the garden He unbuttoned her blouse, unhooking the white bra and exposing twin towers with pink tips. They looked too delicious to be left alone so Bud put his mouth on one, just massaging it to stiffen it. Thank goodness the condoms came in twos; he had one in his billfold, like every teen aged boy.

Before he knew it, the screen disappeared as he was lying on her; the skirt was up and her silken panties were off AND he was spearing her. She moaned and spoke in unknown tongues as they were in rhythm in the fleshly melding. When he slowed, April did also and it subsided to a silence.

As they drove to the campus, Bud said "what a movie" as April punched him on his arm. They were an item on campus but there were so many romances, beginning and ending that no one noticed. NOW it was really difficult to talk to Morgan; even one of strong fiber had trouble speaking rationally to two women alternatively. She would catch on soon but wouldn't it be better to tell her? No, he thought, not over the phone; this girl, whom I still love, but am a p---y hound, deserves better. Now that Bud had debauched this lovely girl at her tender age of 16; running wild with another; he had to finally do the right thing. But what was that? Only praying could give him the answer. He must seek peace.

Bud thought 'it's not that I'm at love with April but I admit that I can't make it without a woman; going downtown is not the answer as I can get anything from those girls. So, can I work it out with Morgan? Not likely; she's a one- man girl and he had better be the same'. Bud, out loud "I have to tell her soon and let the chips fall where they may". So, he planned to go home before February was over and meet any trouble coming from the other way.

He still called Morgan nightly; since he had made the decision, he felt relieved. Now he had to tell April who was beginning to fall for him. Two whammies back to back; what if he lost them both? Not much advantage in having two women, strong-willed, independent, fiery and capable of giving a man more than he could handle. He was seeing April tonight; a buddy was out of town and his apartment was the place for the date. They got there fairly early, sat and listened to music; very nice as they snuggled on the couch. A bit of petting took place as she breathed harder just massaging his tool. He took most of her clothing off, marveling at her trim body and nice breasts. She shed the rest standing before him like a goddess. She lay on the couch as he skinned out of his clothing; reaching for her privates, hidden in a mass of black hair. They indulged each other sexually in any way known to him. As they rested, Bud knew that this was the time to tell her. Bud "Morgan knows that I'm dating so I need to come clean with her".

April "what does that mean? What will you tell her?" B "Everything about you and me; she deserves to know that I'm unfaithful". A "You're not engaged or married; I fail to see it". B "There is no way that a man can go with two women at the same time without big trouble". April "I think you're saying that the man or one woman has to make a choice". B "you got it; I have no idea how bad she'll take it but the pressure is getting to me".

April "I understand; you have to settle with her; she's young and can get over it quickly but you and I are here". Bud agreed with her but he was reluctant to hurt his first love as he still loved her. How does he express to April and Morgan his true feelings? Sex was a large thing but being able to converse and interact with a lady was so, so important. Can't April understand, Bud thought?

April "I don't care if you date or screw or whatever as long as you treat me as nice as you do". Bud "I appreciate that; but I doubt if Morgan can be that generous". April "Bud, you have to do your best; I'll be here regardless". Listening to more soft music, we quietly eased back into a romantical mode, kissing, feeling, thinking sexually. Bud admitted that he liked sex more than most and April could certainly hold her own in it. She reached for his zipper, opening his trousers, displaying a tangle of reddish hair and length of rigid flesh, which she seized as if a prize. Bud knew her procedures for sex, permitting her to go the route. She did even when fellatio wasn't all that cool. This episode took at least 25 minutes s both were covered with sweat when both climaxed.

Bud called afterwards to Morgan to tell her he'd be there tomorrow to talk to her; she agreed to meet him shortly after he arrived. In the AM he left at 8 and it took about 21/2 hours as it was hard to get a 4 lane-road to Prosperity. He drove promptly to Morgan's house; she left school early. He knocked on the door; she almost jumped into his arms as they kissed, both swearing their love for each other.

Bud said "Can we take a drive?" M "How about the creek?" He looked at her and smiled; she returned the smile. They left before noon for their favorite place, parking around 1130A. Bud started "Morgan I've been out with someone; it started as a tutoring relationship and progressed". Morgan "Did you have relations with her?" Bud "I did". Morgan stated crying, "I thought that we were a pair with no room for others". B "I never planned to hurt you but her approach was direct and effective; her sexual pull was effective".

Morgan "We must be strong to avoid the temptations of sex; I did it and hoped that you would". Bud "I couldn't or didn't". Morgan "what do we do now?" B "that's why I'm here, what do you say?" Morgan "I can't lose you because of sexual matters; men usually have more drive than women so I can understand how it happened". Bud "what do you want to do?" Morgan "Try to go on as before; I'll come up every other weekend so that you don't have to have relations with any other". B "Can you do that?" M "I'm sure going to try; we only have 3 more months until you'll be back". Bud was relieved; she was some girl. He reached for her as she reached for him; the merry go round was moving. Afterwards, they rode back to her house and just sat and talked.

The next day, Bud woke up early, ate his breakfast and went to say goodbye to Morgan. Bad news, he knew, but nothing else would work. Arriving there, she came out; they sat on the garden bench, talking about anything except leaving. Finally, it got to him as he stood, said "Morgan, I must go but we've worked it out and I plan to see you there in 10 days or so". She "Bud, you can't go; we still need to talk more". He shook his head, allowing that it would only be worse if he stayed. She then stood, kissed him, running into the house. He drove off without looking back. On the way to UGA he thought of the load off him but feared his meeting with April. He wanted to see her immediately after arriving at the campus. He called her on the cell; she was at the dorm and asked him to come by. When he arrived, she was in the lobby; they sat on a bench as he briefly informed her where things stood. April took it well, admitting that things had been tense, Bud "it's been fun but things are as they ARE. She nodded, kissing him, running upstairs while crying. Another injury by me, thought Bud as he departed. Back at his dorm, he mulled everything over, still sad about the results.

He did not call that night but did the following evening; she answered with her melodic voice. She was tentative as she inquired "did you get everything straightened out?" Bud "yes, it's terminated; I'm expecting you next week". She, perking up "wonderful, Bud, I'll come Friday afternoon, do you have some place where I can stay?" Bud "yes, I know some Sorority girls, Chi Omega, who have an extra bed". M "fine, see yah Friday around 3P if I don't get lost. I think I have it, I75 to Forsyth, Madison, Athens, circular highway to the campus; I'll call when I pass Madison". Bud "Bye darling".

School went on as the pendulum in Edgar Allen Poe's masterpiece; just waiting to sever our heads with the Quarterly exams. I felt its breeze as it passed over my neck. Morgan arrived, was settled, and we walked the campus; it was massive, with great oaks, long leaf pines and azaleas large as trees. The sorority and fraternity houses resembling libraries in their sizes and architecture. Then we both went for our baths, dressed, ready for the evening. There was this eatery, music center, hangout called 'Buddys' just off the campus; we started there, running into some jocks from the team. Introducing Morgan, Bud thought 'they might think that she's my younger sister' but so what?" Morgan fit it, she talked not of high school but handled herself well. We ate, danced a set or two then bid the gang a fond adieu. There was another place nearby, the Shark Tank, where the nerds and scholars hung out, debating the average size of navels in the Congo. Morgan liked the ebb/flow of the conversations, at times, picking up on the lingo as a student. Bud was amazed but held his tongue; if she could hold her own, so be it.

After these experiences, Bud took her to the Sorority, where a man could go into a room if escorted by a lady. We fit. We entered her room, locked the door and began the exploration. It came out as usual; there was a bath in the room so we tidied up. I said goodnight and departed.

The rest of the weekend I ushered Morgan around the campus, to the stadium, the great library and more of UGA's older buildings erected throughout its glorious 150 year -old history. It was in operation for some period before the Georgia boys marched off in the Civil War. BG Thomas Cobb, a resident of Athens, killed at Frederickesville, Virginia by a sniper on the left flank of his unit on the slope of Mayre's Hill. He had been one of the drafters of a New Constitution for Georgia as well as a guiding hand for UGA.

Morgan's trips were regular as she had stated and Bud shied away from unattached ladies of whom there were scores. At UGA the females were 14 K and the gents 11K; it didn't take a math genius to calculate that there was over 1 lady for each male. Bud gave up his 11/4 lady for the one he loved.

Football practice began around 20 March, right after Spring break; there would be 25 days of punching each other, tackling in the open field and for the Q Backs, throwing to fast receivers breaking every way, Bud's skills were good but more was needed; this team was designed for perfection, not just 'good'. He worked at it constantly but it was difficult to improve on a system drilled into one. Finally, after 20 days or so, Bud met with the Offensive Asst. Coach, informing him that he might be better at another position AND suggesting guidance. The Coach understood, giving Bud a few thoughts. "Bud, you might think about offensive flanker or receiver; we'll see about your speed". "can you run 100 meters now; do you feel ok?" B "let's get with it". They only had to go outside to the track with a stopwatch. As Bud was at the starting line, the Coach had the stop watch, telling Bud that he would count 1, 2,3 slowly, Bud should get a jump start for the distance used for the trial. It went as agreed; Bud quickly got his speed up to the max and gave it his all to it. The Coach" Bud, I can't believe this watch; it was 10.8 seconds, as fast as any receiver that we have. Tomorrow, report to the receiving corps".

He called Morgan that evening, all excited, about his new position. She jumped for joy, excited about his spirits. They had a time celebrating. The remainder of Spring practice was a breeze; in the intra-squad game, he started as flanker for the Reds. The game ended 10-7 Reds.

The remainder of the school went smoothly; Bud's grades improved greatly. He went home for the Summer wondering about a job; his Dad felt that he needed to get experience in another field but what? The Mill had a large amount of accounting to be done so Bud's Dad asked Morgan's Dad if they could use Bud? They agreed so one day after his return to Prosperity, he was at the mill working. As expected, he was given minor chores to begin but progressed rapidly to more important issues. Morgan was to student teach again, something that she was good with. With both working, their together times must be coordinated. And they did. Time went by and both saved their money; it was always nice to NOT have to ask a parent for social $$.

Sometimes, they would be together at one house or the other, just talking or planning for the future. Morgan would be a Senior and she counted on going to Athens to watch Bud play; would she go to UGA? She wrestled with it but shied away from very large schools. That meant that she and Bud would be a distance apart for at least two years. It was hard growing up and having the tough decisions to tackle BUT that's life. She at east had the three Summer months to decide; it was Emory in Atlanta, Mercer, Valdosta State or Southwest Georgia. Only Emory and Mercer were within a short distance from Athens so Valdosta St. and SW Georgia were out; there was Ga. State College For Women, Milledgeville (ugh, barf) so that's out. Which was it, Little Princess? It wasn't easy to drive from Macon (Mercer) to Athens but you stayed off the Interstate Highways. Would Marsha think that Morgan was copying her? No, not a chance.

Still rolling the choices around, Morgan bore down on the teaching, getting with the lazy ones. Homework was introduced and if not done, grades were affected. If not a pass, the next semester would be necessary. These active loafers got the message now.

The summer rolled on into late August, reporting time for Bud. One last night at the creek was in order and they seized the opportunity. One last Summer fling for these two; they made the best of it. Within 2 weeks, Morgan started her Senior year; her Freshman class was 60 but it was now down to 40. Marriages, moving, the Army; all contributed to the losses. Also affected the number of teachers authorized; they had to shift around to cover more subjects.

The Fall flew by; Morgan went to 3 UGA home games and a couple of other weekends, Bud was playing well, actually getting a bit faster. They used the sorority setup when they could and a motel when they had to. Football was over and Christmas was here. Bud came home as enthusiastic as ever: when one was in the dumps, the other felt it, similar to the Siamese Chinese, Ying and Yang. The school had social events and Bud joined in, wearing his red/black football jacket like a Champ.

As one gets older, the pleasant moments seem to pass rapidly. Such was the holiday season; before Bud pulled off his jacket, it was time to return. Morgan had breakfast that morning with Bud; then it was up, up and away. Their sadness was becoming numb as they had gone through so much. After the leave from school, Morgan got down to selecting a college but it wasn't easy. Geography was the major eliminator, as she and Bud would both go back and forth. She even looked at Bessie Tift at Forsyth, incorporated in some years past by Mercer. Forsyth was the pits so scratch it. That left Emory and Mercer, both excellent schools, offering an abundance of majors. Morgan planned to seek a History major with a Psychology miner, an excellent combo.

She knew that she must act soon, no later than March, if she was to be accepted. What to do? Macon-Forsyth was a straight shot to Athens as Atlanta (Emory) was a series of large highways, traffic jams and accidents. Her selection was made for her; the Sororities and Fraternities had houses but no overnight stay-ins, at least for now. That suited Morgan. She filled out the application, attached her check to it and used the U.S. Mail.

It was 4-6 weeks before she got a letter back accepting her. NOW her Dad needed to get her a car, one that could weather the constant travel. He was prepared to do so and took her to Cordele to the Toyota Dealer. The Camry was the hot Toyota, a bit snazzy for the young folks. She found a beige one, just what she needed. She drove it home, as proud as a Private with his PFC. She read the book, taking in all the details; her first auto and a good one.

The Spring Quarter flew by and Graduation was on her; she was not sad as she wanted to get on with her career, whatever it was. She wanted to work for the school as before; they needed her so she was hired. Bud came home and also needed a job; was the Mill available? His record was good so he began once more, working in the accounting dept. He knew it front and back and they welcomed him. Once more he and Morgan had to coordinate their work with their social activities. Both vowed that they would go out at least thrice a week and they did. Morgan looked like a $million and no change given. She had matured but just looked better. She had won one trophy this past December in a beauty/talent contest.

The summer was ending before one realized it; time to shop for clothing and other things needed by a student. This time, it was Albany that had a better selection of everything. Morgan and her Mom came home from Daugherty (Darty) County with the Camry loaded to the roof of the car. She didn't know how they dressed at Mercer but her outfits were the most current available. She understood that the girls there also wore athletic shirts, lettered athletic jackets and anything in between. The Frosh had to go two weeks early so Labor Day was reporting time. There were 600 or so new students from a large number of states, almost all had good outstanding records.

The time was spent registering, purchasing books, receiving a dorm assignment (all Freshmen had to reside in the dormitories). Two women rooms w a bath; single beds, tables, lamps and a couch convertible to a bed. Also, linens for the beds was furnished but not towels, mats, etc. All rooms were outside. Mercer was impressive; since I hadn't visited, I knew only what Marsha had told me. There were some classy girls and some handsome guys in our class; the girls from Florida looked especially trendy and seemed a bit older than most. Then the wave hit us, the other 3 classes were now aboard; the dorms filled up, the student center sold out of sweaters, casual wear, shoes and athletic items. The school was contained in one large square, with all instructional rooms, athletic support activities and laboratories contained in the larger square.

The Greeks weren't permitted to 'rush' the newcomers until the 2d week in October; then it was open season on the innocents. I had eyed a couple of Chi Omegas, a very well thought of sorority, the same as the one that assisted me at UGA. I knew nothing about their activities or, in fact, zero about their doings. Bud usually called every other night and we talked about our day's events; he was deep into practice so his recitation of activities was usually short. My roommate was from Valdosta, the hottest place on the universe. She had that Southwest Ga. drawl that exists among many residing in those 45 counties.

It would be October before Morgan could see Athens with all that she had to do; Bud was similar, he was worn out by the weekend and slept and stayed in the athletic dorm. The time flew and the 2d weekend

In October came around; I left around Noon on Friday driving straight through; the squad had gotten off at Noon so Bud was waiting. He had fixed Morgan up with the Chi Omegas (as they were called) for at least Friday night and maybe Saturday night. The members were pleasant to Morgan, likely they thought her a potential pledge.

He dropped me off for a greeting and bath; picking her up at 6:30 P. They did a few places downtown, getting back to the Sorority house at 9:20. She eased Bud by the groups talking in the living room up to her 'digs'. With the door locked, they began to know each other again; the music on to drown out any unusual noises. Bud slipped out to return at 10:00 in the AM; she was dressed casually for any activity. There was much of the campus left to see s they rode around, as Bud described each edifice. What a campus. The older universities in the U.S. were in the Northeast and in the South. Later they stopped at a college hangout, the Gridiron, large as two big circus tents. Not filled at this hour but still noisy. The team was not playing this week so Bud could loaf and show Morgan all.

This place like most quick food locations, prided itself by serving hotdogs and hamburgers in 20 different ways, throwing in fries and malts. No waitresses, go through the luncheon line, ordering as you went. I ordered for us; not so much for Morgan. We ate leisurely while staring at the old photos of Georgia greats, going back to the 20s-30s; many of them playing single-wing football, without a Quarterback. The old three yards and a cloud of dust. There were photos of Frank Sinkwich, with the thick pad on his broken jaw for protection as well as Fran Tarkenton, one of the best ball-handlers ever. Lamar Davis, Wally Butts (who played at Mercer) their coach, Mark Stafford, Q-back, the Detroit Lions, Hershel Walker from Wrightsville Ga; the great Charlie Trippi, and many great linemen who opened the holes for the backs. Let's not forget Vince Dooley, likely the best Georgia coach ever. Exciting to look at them. Only four had their jerseys retired: Sinkwich, a gutsy tailback (the single wing formation); Hershel Walker, the most powerful rusher at UGA; Theron Sapp, Augusta, Georgia, the man who broke the drought after many consecutive losses to Ga. Tech; then the ... great Charlie Trippi, who later led the Saint Louis Cardinals to the NFL Championship. This great wore the number 62, that of a Guard; the rules changed later. Trippi played in '43, then entered the service, returning in '46 to complete his eligibility. He could do it all.

WE took our time, letting the memories of those days settle in our Psyches; referent to be in the presence of those immortals. The girls had gone from short dresses, to minis to, back up to the knees, then up to the ...... in 30 years. The cheerleaders always looked good but their hair styles puzzled us. How did the Salons stay up with the rapid changes of cosmetology? We decided to go to a movie later in the afternoon; saw "FROM HERE TO ETERNITY" with almost ten stars in it. Sinatra, Kerr, Clift, Lancaster, Donna Reed, Ernie Borgnine and a number of backups. This was a bold film for the day-house of prostitution, adultery, sadism, violence with a beer bottle and you name it. But the main scene was on the beach; Debra Kerr and Burt Lancaster; these lovers put themselves in the places of the persons in the book (FHTO ETERNITY).

They finished the movie and, weariness got both of them. Bud took her to her dwelling, kissed her at the door, and both got a nice night's rest. In the Am Bud waited till 10 to go for her; he took her to the Waffle House, the best waffles in Georgia (and S.C.); they took a booth, talked softly, actually chewed their food as the Big Gorilla sat in their booth. Her need to go back was the only touchy part of the trip BUT it was what it is. They returned to the Sorority. Bud retrieved her things, saw her to her car, kissed her, told her to be careful; then he left at the same time.

On the way back she had plenty of time to think; could Bud not come to Macon? But if he did, it might cost a fortune with motels, meals out, auto expense; as well as the inconvenience of staying off campus. Were there any easy ways to get together? Not in Macon this year; next year she could have an apartment perhaps near the campus. Morgan admitted 'Athens is a more exciting place and the Sorority setup, no overnights, puts a crimp in the plans. Bud and I need to work this out soon. She studied Sun night, trying to prepare for her AM classes. Monday was a blue day but she muddled through. Time flew till the holiday Season, Mercer let out 15 Dec and UGA on the 16th. Both got home in record time; both households lit up like New York. It was great to get back to where you knew what was what.

Both had learned to sleep at every opportunity; catching up on missed time in the land of Nod. They both awoke before noon, searching for a glass or water or milk. She called Bud" Honey may we ride to our creek, just to look at all the greenery?" Bud "our minds are connected; I was thinking the same thing". He continued" I'll be there in 20 minutes". And he was. Both of these fine young people were living their lives as most wish that they could. He parked, without saying anything just pulling her to him, easily done. They kissed, he touched her in a sensitive place; M "whew ". He removed her blouse, there was nothing underneath except flesh that he kissed. She was excited" I need you, Bud" as he held her. Bud slowed down as he did not want to become only fascinated with her physically. M "is everything ok, Bud?" Bud "it's fine but I'm just a bit tired; but being with you perks me up" "I like to talk to you as much as anything." Things cooled down.

She was at his house that afternoon, talking to his folks, watching the fire, trying to think what she could her parents and her love. She had some $ as she spent nothing at school, tutoring from time to time. Hmmm, let's see for Dad; a tie rack to replace the hanger that he used; Mom, a magnetic wall fixture for her knife set to rest upon. How about Mr. Big? What does one give a jock who has most everything? Let's see, she thought of a sweater, Ext Lg, Alpaca. The clerk asked "where do the Alpacas live?" Morgan," close to the Peruvians". Sale made.

Why did vacation speed by as school was like pouring frozen syrup through a sieve? Bud and I spent at least half of our awake time with our parents, surprising them about our unselfish attitudes. Now we were on a higher plateau between the mature individual and the maturing young adult. We were viewed as equal conversationalists and our opinions were sought on most household decisions and especially on some economic issues; Bud/I had really learned some economics in our first extended residences, requiring measurements and concern about money.

We found time for ourselves; the valued creek still had its attractions beyond a sanctuary for sex by ascending young people. We wondered if 'our' place could be a secret for very long? Adopting the phrase 'what is, IS' we continued our visits but Bud's (or Morgan's) golden coin sealants were always destroyed elsewhere.

Morgan sought activities with her Mom and Dad, as their schedules permitted, shopping, lunch, bridge, all bonding methods. Of course, there was time for Bud; his desires were not unusual but certainly robust. Morgan felt likewise but when he and she were some distance removed, her energies transferred to her required duties. There was sufficient time for them to indulge their desires, cementing their troth and maturing their relationship.

She saw Bud's parents often, still wondering about something for them as presents; this was hard. She knew not their variety of toys so had to wing it. Not too big and not too small for these great people. She went to the best pharmacy looking at the selection. Ugh. Mostly plastic with shiny, metallic stands. She found a sachet packet with the scents of nature embedded. Its use was in the small purse, available to her at all times. It was perfect, especially with a lady who was so busy as to complete her toilette'. Now for the Dad. A gift for all; a men's manicure set, with several nail clippers, a small file and a cuticle remover. All these for $25.00; talk about savings.

The last chore before Christmas. The night before Christmas, Bud came over; they sat around the fireplace, telling anecdotes about their issues in high school, unheard before by her Mom and Dad. The largest issue was when she was a Jr. In the Prosperity Beauty/Talent Contest. Her dress was new and pretty but she had only tried it once. It, of course, zipped up the back, requiring another to zip it. Just before she was scheduled to go out before the judges, one tried to zip her gown up; it balked so she used force; you know, breaking off a couple of prongs from the intersecting parts. The fastener of the zipper parts was unable to fasten this break together. The cry went out "safety pins to the front"; all sought something to 'get' the gown through the event. A pin or two were found and a stapler was thrown in. The problem was solved for a time but Morgan had to face the audience all the time; she could not turn her back to the front. She won first place that night, the fourth of her victories in the beauty contests; her competition was good but her pleasant demeanor, calmness with the questioning and her singing of "Danny Boy" were too much for the others.

The Holiday Season is better for those who reside away, but visit with close relatives and friends. Seeing these daily or frequently does not excite one during the tear or at the Season. Morgan was grown for all intents; ready to select a career and get on with it. She was taking a History class every Quarter and two Psychology courses this year. Christmas night was clear and cold; they were at Bud's house opening presents with his Dad and Mom. Morgan received a cashmere sweater, Bud a set of luggage as Morgan presented her presents to them. All raved over their gifts, exclaiming how could anyone have such perfect judgment. Then they went to her house, for the other 'gifting'. They all unwrapped gifts, sitting around the fireplace, really not desiring anything beyond the companionship.

In the AM Bud came by as Morgan was having her breakfast; he sat just talking quietly to her. She finished, wiped her lips and gave him a big kiss, full lips, pressure, all the bells and whistles. He accepted, hugging her like a bear, as he started leaving. She trailed, catching him at the door for a repeat performance.

She did not follow him to the car; that could be sadder for both. He drove off slowly, looking back to see her one more time. She had to be back on the 2d but what would she do with this7 days? She COULD not just sit around Prosperity; waiting for what or whom? Her Dad said that she could work at the Mill with a skeleton staff, filing, copying, typing, just tidying up for the new year. She leaped at it; the hours were 8-4, just right. Starting Dec 27, for five days.

These days filled the void; she had her nightly talks with Bud, and just watched TV or worked with her computer. She tried not to eat too much but her Mother was determined to, as she called it "just take the wrinkles out". Not being around the house really helped to keep off the weight. Then it was New Year's Eve, Morgan thought "Silent Night, Lonely Night"' to be apart any of Christmas was the same.

Back on the road on the 2d, Morgan arrived at around 2P at the campus. Morgan unloaded her car and a couple of friends helped her carry all up to her room. Her roommate was already in; they exchanged greetings as Morgan began putting away her possessions. Before she was aware it was 5P the dining hall opened 5:15; she needed to go early and come back to make her bed; not to mention, go to bed early as 8A comes early. They went to the DH, got in line as the Army, and got their trays. No waitresses here. The food was almost good but did save on your money if you ate elsewhere. Back at the dorm, girls were relating their adventures of December as many of us were just trying to get our rooms in order.

In the AM and the week, hitting the books to try to gain on her courses, Morgan was busy, only breaking for Bud's call. Nothing except needing, missing and wanting, was so important. Surprisingly, Winter Quarter usually produced the better grades; the early darkness, lack of activities and settling down of the classes brought their GPAs up. Morgan had two As and one B, the Dean's List. Her Major and Minor were humming along. There was a brief Spring break and she went to Athens for two days; they just explored the areas around Athens, trying not to spend money that they could not spare. In the smaller towns, prices were much more moderate so they stayed there two nights.

She began her final quarter of the year on a high note, Bud was in Spring practice and she had her nose towards the books. Then it came, the final days of May, the end was 31 May; another removal of personal gear to her home. She was on the road for Prosperity, a bit older and wiser. They greeted her as her car slid under the porch roof.

She met them with large hugs; trying to forget her packed car. They said "don't worry, we'll help with it". The next AM she called the school; there were 3 students needing tutoring AND could pay. She took them all on, fortunately they had the same subjects. Beginning the next day, she was on her usual schedule of 0830-Noon. She was used to it so their small class zipped along for 5 weeks; then two more came forth needing help, the Summer was occupied. Bud got home within the week to seek again employment by the mill; they had something for him. It was a struggle by college students to find work; almost all needed it. We were fortunate and knew it.

We had the later afternoons and nights to mingle; but curfew was early, no later than 10P. Of course, to us who lived by the clock at school, these hours were heaven. We stuck to our memories of the creek, going there every chance that we had if I was not under the weather. Not indulging ourselves with spending, our bank accounts grew, giving us a sense of security. We rarely ate out and then, only a quick sandwich. It was hot as blazes most of the time, cooling off a bit in the late PM with the rains; not only the farmers wanted the rains.

Morgan was lucky in that she had better students than usual; they had been dilatory in their studies and only needed a 'prodding' that she could give them. They DID appreciate the opportunity of being able to join their classes this September. It was no easy task to go to school in the Summer as thoughts of others at the beach, Disneyworld, or in the mountains. One summer school was usually enough for the strongest.

September was approaching and Morgan needed to pick up a garment or so for this year; they decided that Tifton was the place to look; Morgan had not been there for several years so, relished the thought. This town on I-75, the agricultural center of SW Georgia, was growing; several ladies boutiques, as well as men's shops. We sought items to match up with my wardrobe, not expensive but handy.

CHAPTER VI: ONWARD

Back on campus, she still stayed in the dorm; it was simpler, cheaper and more convenient. Her roommate was gone, but she snagged a friend who was solo. Her classes were art, psychology and biology (ugh). She had to have these so, bite the bullet. Morgan hit the ground running with her eyes on the goal, to make good grades and mow down the required courses. Bud was in the mix but Fall quarter was the time to press the issue. No football at Mercer unless one watched it on TV; Fall quarter was better for studying unless you had your friend handy. And Morgan didn't.

The Holidays approached, Mercer was out 15-2d and UGA 16-1st; plenty of time for socializing OR. She drove home on the 15th arriving in early afternoon. Mom and Dad awaited, meeting her in the driveway; a great reunion. They chatted that night by the fireplace, just in a casual manner, maybe mentioning a few friends who remained local. In the AM she called the school, arranging her tutoring duties, 3 the first 5 weeks and 2 the final course prior to Sept. Their courses were almost identical so Morgan was not required to familiarize herself with more books. She started promptly for the period 0830-Noon. They were eager; if they didn't pass this course, they could be held back. A fate worse than hanging.

Bud came in that afternoon; a couple of hours with his family then over to see Morgan. He stayed awhile at her house, then suggested a ride in the country. Morgan looked sideways at Bud, who kept a straight face. In the car riding, Morgan "How could you do it with a blank face, you satyr?" But Bud could think/concentrate better at the 'creek' and Morgan had begun to understand. Yes, two young people in love are naturally attracted to the physical side of the relationship BUT Bud used his restraint and maturity to make their relationship more than that.

Both were at work the next morning; he at the Mill and Morgan at school. They tried to have lunch together and did, at times. The Summer flowed on reaching September; time for the scholars to go back. She to her Junior year and Bud for his last Quarter; football had cost him that time. He was taking his final Accounting course as well as Computers; then graduation but before, a search for a job. While employed, he could study for the CPA Exam, the pinnacle for accountants.

Back at Mercer, Morgan continued History courses as well as some Psychology studies. She had been exempted from the foreign language requirement as she had two years in high school. Morgan was up on all requirements so she took Art and Economics. She was receiving a well-rounded education, enabling her to socialize or deal with professionals on their leval. She learned that Mercer-Weslyn were planning a Beauty/Talent contest the latter part of October; each entry had to be sponsored by a Mercer entity. Who would sponsor her? She knew some Fraternity guys, a few ATOs, some Phi Delts, and a couple of SAEs. Since she knew the ATOs better, she approached one, telling him that she planned to run. He talked to the members who agreed to sponsor her. She had a great gown so no expense.

The Quarter flew by to the last week in October; the fraternity stood behind her as the number grew of applicants; many from Mercer and quite a few from the Ladies College. Morgan felt like 'Danny Boy' was as good as any other tune. The night came with 22 ladies enrolled; the Judges were prepared as they asked each Lady a few questions, had each walk forward and to in front of the Judging table. The final test was the talent, often the weakness of most contestants. There was a variety of presentations, some not so good; The singers were few but good. As the trials ended, there was a head gathering of the Judges. They selected 7 to come back out, Morgan among them. More questions and for a couple, a few bars of their songs. They huddled and then, 4 were let go; Morgan stayed. In the end Morgan won and took home her 5th Beauty/Talent prize.

Christmas was here; Bud found a position in Macon with a large Accounting firm, starting in January. He had a few days in mid -December in Prosperity so they could spend a few days together. Very brief as he had to take some state tests before working. Morgan felt about it but it was his future so that's it.

She stayed around her house, not going anywhere. Bud was there for a few days but time flew. She did tutor and that was some relief. There were no Christmas gatherings that year. She did get presents for all four parents but didn't spend the time picking them out that she had before. Let's see, tie for Dad, BR shoes for Mom; a reversible belt (blk/bn), and a magnifying glass for Bud's parents. It wasn't the same.

She asked for time to fly a s she spent New Year's Eve by herself. Dullsville, is what Morgan thought; she was correct. Finally, the sun lifted and she headed for Macon. The dorms or at least one was opened early, so she had shelter. A few girls were there so they made friends quickly. Most were upper class women, so the conversation was mature. Most had boyfriends tied up with work or foreign travel. No one complained as we all ate the mush.

Classes started and Morgan jumped ahead with her advance study of her courses; the Profs weren't used to that. This was a short quarter and it zoomed by. Bud was in town and they met on the weekend IF he had not been sent out of town by his employer. Spring was there and the Quarter began on March 20. Bud was getting into his routine and cutting down a bit on his travel; he liked the job and was learning a lot. She decided to stay at the school during the break so she and Bud could have some time together; he had an apartment on a direct line from Mercer, On College Avenue from the school about a mile, his apartment was close to the Mercer Law School, on the hillside, overlooking the Ocmulgee River. These were hard to come by so Bud was fortunate. Morgan brought her clothing, other personal items and christened the apartment. Her first night there was unusual to her; it was as if she and Bud were married. Morgan felt that way, resenting forward guys hitting on her, but realized that they didn't know. Other guys were afraid to ask her out because of her beauty and sophistication. She WAS satisfied with her choice.

Morgan was playing house as Bud made the living; they did not go out but one night to the 1786 Inn, only a couple numbers down College Street; not cheap but Bud wanted to do something for me. The food unlike anything we'd had; melted in the mouth. The wine, a black French Allain, was smooth, mellow and intriguing to the taste. Where did Bud learn to choose a wine, thought Morgan? He said "on the road, I constantly ask the waiters what wine goes with what; they inform me". Morgan laughed "can you read my mind?" Bud" not any more than you can read mine but I saw you looking at me when I ordered".

The Inn was definitely Revolutionary War designed; actually, there when the War was on. Georgia had almost no contact with the British as the fighting was along the Atlantic Coast. Nice restaurant.

The nights were nice and comfortable; to sleep the whole night with the one whom you loved, was so exciting and comforting that she felt that she'd never be insecure again. She found out if he snored;

he didn't, did she? The week was over too soon and she needed to get back to the dorm. But now she knew the landscape and could stay when it was convenient.

Spring Quarter flew during her Junior year; she did well in her subjects, despite pining for Bud at times. Her maturity enhanced her abilities to absorb more within the brain in less time, than the younger students. It looked as if she was smarter but a lot of it was that she 'was quicker'. Whatever, her potential was greater than most.

The school end was coming; she only had the students in Prosperity for income so she had to go home, jobs were few in Macon for students and especially for females. She would not stay in Macon and be a burden on Bud. In another year, she could teach, but now she was in-between. The end of May she spent several nights with Bud; just as wonderful as ever.

Around the first week of June, Morgan retrieved her things from Bud's apartment and started the lonesome journey home. Her parents knew that she was 'down' from the situation so left her alone to work out the darkness. It was a few days before she talked about working; she really liked the tutoring so she started again with the students. No trouble with any but boys are boys. Of course, most of these kids were raised on farms or knew how to hunt or trap. Blood was not a stranger to them, neither was a bit of violence. Fighting, whether on the sports fields or not, was not uncommon. Her students were entering the area of taunting females, even to the point of touching them but had never shown her those traits.

The summer flew by but the boredom continued. She talked to her 'man' every night BUT what can one say about tutoring negligent students? She even fabricated interesting stories to keep up his interest. His voice was confidant and pleasant; he passed his CPA exam; that called for a large raise. Every little bit could move their marriage closer and that was most pleasant.

She was preparing to return to Mercer for her final year; glad but unsure about her employment future; ladies could teach, be nurses, secretaries, maybe Pharmacists but what else? She knew teaching and there would always be a job for her; insecurity again reared its ugly head. She needed to apply by January 1998, to obtain a position at a school with the better students.

Back at the dorm, the nose in the books; the GPA did account for a bit when seeking a job. Morgan's spirits rose since Bud was just a mile down the street but they both had duties to perform, not leaving a large amount of time. Time slipped through the hour glass; the busy ones hardly noticed. Morgan was bearing down reaching for the better grades. Bud was in and out, as a salesman; he was the same but his brow began to have a couple of small wrinkles. Morgan was at the top of her game in looks, intellect and personality. Her fellow students admired her determination and good humor; she was very popular.

The holiday season arrived, bringing a small break from studies and the routine; Morgan was at home as Bud was back and forth. They were together as circumstances permitted; the old spark was there and they participated willingly. She decided not to try to find a job this season but just be around the house, reigniting the relationship with her parents. They loved her approach as she assisted her Mom in baking for the church and making up school packs for the less fortunate. In Prosperity there were a number of families not able to afford the basics; the churches and civic groups filled the bill, giving without claiming, coats, jackets, bicycles and toys for the little ones. The presents were from Santa or the parents, the children accepted that.

Bud was home for Christmas Eve so they attended church, the candle-light service, holding hands as teenagers. Afterwards, they rode to the Flint River, to sit in solitude, reflecting on their fortunes. The moon was reflecting off the river as it began to snow. The large flakes stuck on the windshield giving it a delicate pattern with so many flakes.

They did 'neck' or 'pet', whatever the terms were now. Nothing heavy but it wouldn't take long to generate some heat. They were there some time, often without speaking then Morgan "Bud, do you need more freedom on your trips?" Bud "what do you mean, Morgan?" M." you need some freedom to mix with clients, females included. And now and then, an occasion can arise where you have to host a lady at dinner". Bud "you'd be OK with that program?" M "it is practical and eliminates any deception; I might have the same privileges". Bud "you're right, we can't be together as much as desired so some arrangement of freedom must be agreed to". M "both of us must be cautious to avoid any entanglement that threatens our relationship; if it does occur, each must notify the other immediately". B" done".

It wasn't written but was a pact between two romantic friends, trying to preserve a valuable relationship of years by practical rule-making. Not easy but at least an attempt to bring order to a situation that might become strained that intrigue entered the picture. Morgan was becoming wiser and wiser as Bud marveled at her sagacity.

On the way back to town, they chatted as usual, the burden lifted from both their shoulders. He kissed her goodnight "Morgan, I'll be here at 11A if it's OK?" She nodded, she had a nice new document carrier for him. He gave her a cashmere coat; the girls would have navigated the English Channel for that. They sat just thinking when Bud "Morgan I'm joining the National Guard here before long; I haven't done anything for my country and it's about time". Morgan "I don't object but won't it interfere with your job?" B "not really, as its only one night a month plus the 15 days for Summer camp. Actually, every employer must let you go for that w/o cutting your pay". M "I admire you for this and I can still see you at least once a month or more".

Bud was on his way to Macon, a new year was just around the corner; his thoughts shifted to his job, one of the best for a recent grad. Morgan sat silently thinking how things were changing so quickly; and she thought 'once we had it all and now I have to make a 'treaty' against one of us violating the vows to the other'. She wondered if the pact was more for her than for Bud; she knew that men were normally more inclined to be receptive to sex than females BUT not her. She had been tempted several times to go out but that was the first step to coitus.

Morgan shrugged it all off, writing her applications for a teaching job at Tifton, Perry and Prosperity. They promised to respond by the middle of March. Tifton and Perry were chosen for proximity to home and because their students were more likely to be responsible. Prosperity was selected because of economics I.e. nearness to home/ability to save money. The conduct of the students there could be controlled by familiarity with the parents.

Back at school, the grind accelerated as a couple of her last courses were 'bears' with bites. Medieval History was about times unfamiliar to most students and unwanted by the others. Morgan rationalized "this course is just like a diamond, immune to a group of drills until the correct one is applied; I hope that I am the necessary one". She normally did not take notes but this was different; a small recorder was brought in with her handbag and she took notes on the large issues. Later to fill them out with the recording. Good girl.

There was another girl in the class known to be 'sharp' so they agreed to join together on their studies. It was unlikely that the course could whip both of them.

She had another Psychology course, self-denigration, or a persecution complex, a common illness where the victim (on her own) decides that some or many are torturing her for no reason.

The Winter, with its rain, glided on by the dedicated students, inching towards the finish line, graduation, around 1 June or so. Morgan got replies from the 3 high schools, where she had applied. All were approving of her qualifications; Tifton said that their staff remained intact as there were no turnovers; Perry said essentially the same but had two prior teachers to return this year. Prosperity was ecstatic about obtaining a hometown teacher; that is a rare occasion. They mentioned not the pay, but Morgan knew about the scale; a few counties paid more. Her boarding situation was favorable, permitting her to save a fair amount of her pay. She needed to report by August 1.

Was Morgan pleased? She called Bud that night letting him in on it. It was pleasing to him as they would be together at a minimum of one day a month. He had joined within the past week; it was an Engineer company.

She thought that life had been rapid before; well, it had speeded up. The Spring break was short so she stayed with Bud for 2-3 days before going home for a couple of days. Her parents were pleased about her new job. While home, she called on Bud's parents after 5P. They were always cordial and talkative, raving about his new military service. They were proud of Morgan and Bud, both homegrown, venturing into the complicated world. Bud was moving in his job; his ability with figures was astonishing. We'll always need CPAs thought Morgan; men will keep messing up lines of numbers as long as there are lines.

Now it was the final climb to the sheepskin, rather the parchment; Morgan was surprised that one had to pay for that also. She wondered when air would require a deposit. The finals were completed and grades were calculated. She qualified for Cum Laude honors, no slouch this Prosperity girl; she has a different colored tassel from most. She thought so the ones in the balcony could throw popcorn at her. Monday arrived and all were decked out for the formalities, some 300 graduates scattering to the ends of the earth to cement their careers. When the name was called along with the honor if any, the person moved forward, accepted the diploma, mumbled something or not, then swung out the auditorium. It was loud out there as the crowd was commending the graduates; it was brief for photos, then cleared as rapidly.

Back home, without her cap/gown, that was turned in prior to leaving the campus, Morgan reflected on her last four years; the costs, the effort, the stress and the friends, the friendships and the memories. AS Dean Martin sang “Memories are made of this”; Morgan had only an instant of doubt about her abilities to succeed in this world; they all had worked hard to make it this far but now she was a bit insecure, one of her few questions about herself.

She did everything by rote for a day or so, quiet and reflective; her Mother worried a bit about her but felt that she could make it with her inner strength. And she did. Talking to Bud eased the tension as he put the matter in perspective “Morgan, you’ve been so brave for so long that you can’t relax when the big task is completed; you will ease up in a day or so, enjoying the fruits of your labor. So, my darling, I salute you for navigating one of the better colleges in Georgia; believe me, your efforts are noticed and applauded”. She felt better, sleeping until 9:30 A in the morning.

What will she do until August? There was still a need for tutoring and she now had the full credentials. There was a need and she could do it. Going to work was healing; she dove in, teaching these kids how to concentrate on the important; as the saying went ‘accentuate the positive; eliminate the negative’. She had never been more complete as the pupils grasped matters never reaching their minds before.

She had the afternoons, trying to remember when Bud came. He called the night before, alerting her to the Guard meeting and his trip around Noon. She was free after the class, awaiting his arrival at home; he came so silently that she was off guard.

CHAPTER VII: TURNING THE PAGE

They rode around, catching up on each other's news; Bud was travelling, mostly in Georgia so their meetings were not frequently. They didn't seem as close but this was natural for two who were apart so much, both under constant stress. They tried to be light about it all, shaking off the doubts by joking and parody. Sooner or later, the tenseness would be pierced by a bit of reality. Bud joked "Morgan, want to ride to the creek for a while? Morgan, silent for a bit "No, Bud I don't think so; we need to know each other better". Bud, hurt "what's wrong?" M "what's right?" He knew then that things had changed; it could never be the same; separations rarely are good for a relationship "I'm beginning to understand how you feel; I'm sorry to take or imply any control over you; it has been bad for both but you have suffered more. Let's part now, meeting in the future when time has, hopefully, healed your wounds". He dropped her at her home, as considerate as ever. Like a book, the pages were turning.

The trash was now in the stew; it was necessary to get it out; Morgan had wondered if she could reach the point of speaking her conscience. There might not be a culprit; circumstances, unplanned, was the catalyst of the division of two. Regardless, it is useless to try to affix blame for an inevitable result; yes, thoughts of it were so paralyzing that both had omitted it from their thought processes. This pressure release would, in time, be beneficial to each.

Morgan, thankfully, had her work; each day she developed the energy to deliver to these youngsters, the guidance needed for their successful progress to the next grade. Time flew, as always, when one was gainfully employed with worthy endeavors. She had lunch, usually, at home, then took a ride in the country just to clear her head; the sight of the green rows of peanuts, soybeans and cotton as well as higher stalks of corn, were proof of the massive capacity of this Southwest Georgia to feed the states East of the Mississippi River. They grew two types of peanuts: Spanish, the smaller, grew in a clump AND Runners, that did, as described, putting out ground vines, that produced larger peanuts; the vines from the adjacent rows helping fill in the row middle

Since none knew of her 'breakup', Morgan was undisturbed by males as she moved towards the August date for full employment. It had been some time since a male had approached her romantically so she was, at the present, under their radar. Her thoughts were focused on the healing that is necessitated by this traumatic event. Others are unable to accomplish this for her; it is individual in nature, only mitigated by her maturing thought of the betterment for both.

Her duties were well done; her check was welcomed and she began to resolve the uncertainties within her mind. Her smile returned, enlightening all that the Morgan was recovering. AS her stress decreased, her vitality increased, encouraging her parents. Most were unaware of this situation, thinking that Morgan was just worried about her future; whereas, she was to a large degree, entwined in the past.

Bud had returned to Macon, thrown himself into his exacting job, travelled frequently and tried, himself, to erase the anguish from his mind. He knew that it was not easy but had to reach this ultimate solution.

August arrived and Morgan had her first day as a teacher. No students were there, as this was pre-planning, to try to anticipate the requirements of the students during the following nine months. She was introduced, but many knew her already; she was easily the youngest of the faculty. The sessions were mostly half-day so they were not so demanding; Morgan would teach History and Psychology to the Seniors and others. The age differential between this teacher and Seniors was at the most four years, not a large span for the male-female relationship.

Morgan had to attire herself differently for her duties; not that she was ever improperly dressed before, however, the stares of older students necessitated that she be as demure as possible. She was professional, demanding thorough preparation for her classes; but always explaining fully the issues of the lesson. There were 2 Senior classes, of 30 each, so each student was able to receive help if he/she required it. There were no disciplinary problems at present as, it seemed, the students were trying to determine if she was real. She was and wanted only to teach them the best of her subjects.

The quarter moved along; the football games, pep rallies and dances after the games, filled the after-hours; the teachers were on duty at the refreshment stand, the dances and, at times, the rallies. Morgan did, if not working, attend a few games but everything brought her in contact with her students. They began to know her, Ms. Mitchell, AKA the Mercer Beauty Queen. They knew more about her than she knew about them but that was usual.

A couple of guys were in the Guard here, seeing Bud at every drill; putting Bud with Morgan, hmmm, what is going on? They were nice enough to avoid asking about it, however, 'it' was in the air. How does one, if at all, try to explain something that was so good for 6 years, then unwound in a brief span? You don't in a position like this. Morgan put it out of her mind.

The school still had a good football team but no leader like Bud; their leadership was not up to the past. Hard playing but when it got tough, there was no one to keep them going. This is the hardest position to fill; few have it and few of these use it. Morgan didn't enjoy these games anymore after that undefeated season with Bud at the throttle.

Fall slid by and 'finals' loomed over her students; how would her test be? Morgan thought along these same lines, how hard should it be? If too hard, then some or more might fail; if too easy, too many would make As or Bs. The school liked the pyramid with a couple or three at the top; 6-8 on the lower tier; maybe 15 or so on the 2d tier from the bottom and 3-4 on the bottom tier. She really didn't like the bottom tier at that level so she designed the test for plusses, C+, B+ and minuses, C- ,B- so the grades would not be bunched. No one should fail, maybe a D or so. One would have to be a gourd to fail.

Nobody fainted when the History exam was passed out; a good sign. The Psychology exam was just multiple choice with NO tricks. This course could lead to a very difficult exam so Morgan had to be extremely careful to proper tailor it to her group. Both classes turned out with only one F each, a miracle. The classes were receptive to her prepared tests; thereby validating her instructional abilities. She left for the holiday break in good spirits but no plans.

At home, she thought about the break; it was nice but she had little to do now that she was off. She was asked to chaperone a hayride and escort a number of students to Tifton for a movie; she said yes to both. The hayride was tougher as those boys/girls could get out of sight under the hay or behind it. Both events were stimulating to her; positive overall. She shopped a bit, always uncertain as to her purchases; in the finality, she bought the best available. For Dad, slippers; for Mom, a new housecoat, the end. Bud was out and I had to leave off his parents due to the situation.

There were a few young adults in town; we gathered and planned a couple of events, fudge making and toy renovation. Collecting used toys, we painted, refurbished and polished the once-used children's presents. Obtaining a list of kids from the Family/Children's Office, we delivered the toys and fudge to the parents who were Santa Claus. Not fancy but beneficial to the community. Most of the group were married but some were unattached. Morgan worked closely with Dave, employed at Georgia Power; he was gregarious, pleasant and very nice to her. The first man that she had noticed in eons. And he noticed her, being so polite and considerate of her. This was still a time when the man had to do the asking but Morgan chafed at this. An idea was present, she knew Jill and Bob who knew Dave well. Was it possible for them to invite both at the same time? Morgan called Jill and 'set' it up for the following weekend; dinner at their house, that's all; the rest was up to her and Dave. On Friday night, Morgan drove over and knocked on the door; Dave opened it and both greeted each other. There was conversation in the family room until 8, then they went into a beautiful dining room. Dinner was great as all just talked their heads almost off. After dinner all adjourned back to the FM; the dessert was great. More talk until 9:30 P when the solitaires were leaving. On the outside, Dave asked if we could go somewhere to talk? Morgan agreed and he said the Elk Club was nice with music and atmosphere. Both drove there and went inside. The lounge was perfect for their conversation.

Dave was a good one for letting the other talk but he could hold up his end. Smooth, not pushy, knowledgeable, not a know it all and travelled. Morgan was impressed; he was a Ga, Tech graduate in electrical engineering. His tickets were impressive; he stayed away from her prior life, leaving it up to her what she wanted to divulge. It was great and Morgan wrote her cell number on a bar napkin for him. He knew that she was a teacher at the high school so they knew a bit about each other from the beginning. Around 11P they decided to leave; Dave asked if he could call her; the answer was 'lease do'.

She drove home thinking "it's not as bad as I thought; there are guys out there who do respect you". They can say what they want, Morgan thought "Southern men are the best or there is no best". At home, the parents were in bed so she sat by the fireplace, musing over this wonderful night. Going to bed 'sugarplums danced in her head' from one of her nursery rhymes. The first thought in her mind in the AM was "would he call or not'? After lunch he did, his pleasant voice "hi, remember me, I'm the guy who bored you last night" Morgan "you know better, where are you?" Dave "at work but thinking about tonight, are you free or inexpensive?"

Morgan "both, we can go Dutch". Dave "not in my hometown; I'd never live it down". Morgan, "what do you have in mind?" D " how about a movie in Tifton?" M "what's on?" Dave "Easy Rider with Dustin Hoffman and Peter Fonda and, I think, Jon Voight". Morgan "I'm ready". D "how about 6:30?" Morgan "10-4, Pal".

She tried to decide what to wear out that evening; nothing slinky or too sexy; just durable skirt and blouse, with their colors, and flats as she was unsure of his height. She did her nails as she had a purpose for that $20 plus tip; also her toes in case she wore open-toed shoes. Her preparation took a part of the afternoon and she did other cleanup measures, Her Mother said "big night?" She replied "it's Dave from the power company; we're going to the movie in Tifton". Mother "good for you".

At 6:29 Dave drove up in his Volvo, made in Sweden I thought, Did he have any frozen blondes in his trunk I wondered? He had on a coat with open shirt; no place around required a tie in the Summer. Opening the door, I decided to introduce him to Mother, Dad was still at the Mill. I didn't know his last name so just said 'Dave and Mom',

That was OK. We left and he opened the door for me to the car. I started the conversation about his car since he had no tie. I knew that there was no Volvo place around here so I threw out the bait "did you go far for the car?" Dave "Albany has a dealer but I preferred the one in Macon". M "I've seen their signs; with so many makes and models, how do you choose?" Dave "like all geeks I take the consumer reports, studying which they think is better; Volvo was their choice and mine". Morgan "the ultimate search for the Volvo?" Dave "you have it".

The car matter settled I asked about GT, his Alma Mater. Dave "harder than advertised; from a small school I had a time my first year. Learning to study efficiently was my challenge but I finally made it by the first quarter of my Sophomore year. It's not so much brains as it is persistence and separating the wheat from the chaff. Tech was in transition, dropping the Textile major; with China, Formosa, the Orient turning out our linens better and cheaper than we could; why fight the momentum?" M "I can see that his Industrial Revolution is having an impact; is atomic energy now a large part of the electrical Major?" Dave "you bet, it's constantly a battle to determine which form of energy is more economical and for HOW long"

Morgan shifted gears to a liberal arts school "will schools as Mercer change rapidly or slowly?" Dave "likely slowly but personal opinions can cloud and at times, influence students' in their personal beliefs, not related to any subjects except to perhaps Politics and Social Studies. For immature minds, the influence of liberal professors can be excessive". Morgan thought, 'another stout Conservative; hooray.'

The movie was 'Midnite Cowboy' with Hoffman and Jon Voight; a comedy from a few years earlier. We laughed and giggled most of the film thru; as we left, Dave thought that we might eat at the Elks Club so we went by. A nice place that served real steaks and fresh vegetables; a piano player was in the lounge as were we. Morgan "I'd like the filet with a baked potato, medium rare". Dave "make it two with tea, please". The music was very good and Dave asked "would you like to dance?" M "you know how to say it". They tried a dance step, a good round motion for those who had not danced before like us. Dave was light on his feet and Morgan, as most ladies, could hold her own. They talked about anything except 'former attachments', which suited Morgan. The steaks arrived and the parties approached them eagerly. No sauce on them and just a brush of butte on the spuds.

She was not cautious about eating so her steak was all taken in. Dave did not toy around, eating like a working man. Finishing, listening to the music, the waitress inquired if they preferred dessert; several items homemade plus ice cream on pie. The latter was the favorite of many including our two. The pie was apple, and the ice cream, vanilla, yum. Both took their time eating slowly and completely.

Riding back home, they conversed about Tifton and its growth to a minor city, agricultural center of the farming area. Before one could blink, Prosperity was in the headlights. He drove to her house saying "it is late so I can come in another time". Morgan thought 'so polite, he knew that the hour was late for this town'. He walked her to the door, just holding her hand tighter as he opened it for her, while saying "such a great time, Morgan, let's do it again soon". Morgan "goodnight Dave, it was nice and we must repeat very soon".

Again, she sat by the fire, thinking of her life; already knowing two very good men. She considered herself fortunate to have these associations; many ladies never connected with even one good man. Now, she knew that 2 dates did not fill the card, but fine dates counted for much more. Still thinking, she did her preps, then tucked it in. Sleep arrived soon for an exhausted young lady.

The next morning after breakfast, she had to buy presents for her parents, but what? Let's see what the town has; a couple of new stores had opened so why not. She saw a reversible belt, blk/bn, that was nice;

Mom was next. Perhaps a shoe tree would do it, thought Morgan. She purchased with her own money; a nice feeling.

Back at home, her cell rang; it was Dave with his cheerful voice. “Morgan, there’s ice skating tomorrow night by professional skaters in Perry; do you think that you can slip away?” Could she, bet on it “Dave how did you know that my dance card for Thursday is open? What time?” D “about 6;15, we need to eat early as the show is 21/2 hours”. Morgan “I’ll be here”. She hung up her phone, thinking “is this the night that he kisses me?” It seems that girls have two thoughts about a late first kiss “does he like me OR is there something wrong with him?” Thinking on “we’ll see tomorrow night”.

Late in the afternoon, she shampooed her hair (no $25 for the salon), dried it, checked her nails, shaved her legs with a raiser (no solution for her). She was on the top of her game but couldn’t let down; a girl had 4 times the items to polish as a man; one out of kilter ruined the punch. It was similar to a man doing his repetitions of exercises but more delicate.

She had just the outfit, a chiffon blouse and a partial leather skirt with short boots. Quite spiffy but trendy. She knew the sound of his Volvo, almost indistinct but with a slight sound. She went to the door just as his foot hit the front stoop. She opened it as his hand was on the screen door. Dave “Hi, you look like a real fan and I resemble a hayseed or door to door salesman”. M “you look like a fan who got off work late”. Dave, laughing “you know that I have only two coats, and wore one the other night”. Both smiled, the levity was good for all and served to break the ice w/o falling through. He helped her into the car, her small sweater in her hand.

It was about an hour to Perry, straight up I 75; before they got there, a restaurant was on the right, the Hook and Line, a fish and seafood place. This might be easier to eat than a spaghetti and Italian menu. Inside, it was crowded but the waitress said the service was fast.

The menu was filled with a multitude of catches, both fresh and salt water. Morgan decided on fried shrimp and Dave on stuffed crabs. Their cocktails were a mixture of crab and calamari. Morgan did not ask what calamari was. Dave was not up on his seafood either. However, they ate like the shipwrecked. The entrees arrived before they wiped their mouths. Diving in, little talking, they looked at each other, smiling as if each knew a secret.

No dessert this night as Morgan always had popcorn at any event. What was a sports contest without popcorn or peanuts? They reached the coliseum about 7:45, 20 minutes till it started. Dave grabbed the tickets, searched for the seat locations and the presentation began. It is impossible to describe accurately the handsome costumes of our stars, brief but catchy. Morgan hadn't seen this before so she was on her toes or feet cheering as a teenager. They did stunt after stunt, each more difficult than the last. Time flew, then the finale just before ten.

On the way home, the conversation was all about the skaters; most of whom started before they were teenagers and would perform in the Olympics if they had not already. Dave pulled up under the large Oak and stopped. Morgan thought, is this it? Dave thought, if I try and she refuses? She slid over to him as his arm rose to hold her. Now or never. He leaned over as she turned up her angelic face; the kiss was well done, not too quick or hard, her lips soft and his tasting like honey. No pretenses now: Dave "I've wanted to do that for so long" Morgan "and I wanted you to do it". They tried again successfully. She went in.

Again, the fire was her refuge to think and clear her mind. She was getting much better after her disaster. Time stood still as she sat, running every detail through her consciousness. It was uncertain when she went to bed but, what was certain was that she had succeeded in recessing her prior involvement into her Hippocampus. Goodnight, fair Maiden

Christmas Eve arrived, Dave came over at 8 for a sandwich and eggnog; Morgan slipped out that morning and purchased a billfold for him.

Was there ever a man who didn't need a billfold? They sat at the table absorbing the chicken salad on toast; the eggnog had a bit of spiced rum. Then to the family room where we sat around the fireplace. After the talking Morgan distributed the presents to all. All said that this gift solved all their problems; they were unable to live without it.

Later the folks went to bed as Morgan and Dave sat by the fire, just talking about the past and the future. It had to come up so let it out; Dave "do you ever see Bud?" Morgan "no but he's deployed now to the Middle East with the local NG". D "would it hurt if I asked a question?" M "I think not; it was some time ago". D. "this is clumsy but I had to know if feelings were still there". M "not feelings as we think, but memories that don't vanish."Dave "I knew that you would tell me if there was still an obstacle to our relationship". Morgan "he'll be a friend for a long time, but he has his life and I have mine. You are in my life".

Dave shortly excused himself to leave Morgan with her thoughts; she led him to the door, placing a great kiss on him. Dave responded, saying "Morgan I care for you; thanks for including me. I'll call tomorrow".

He called the next day to see if she had time to just ride around as the snow was on the ground. She agreed and they rode out to a mill pond where the kids were trying to ice skate. Since the pond didn't freeze over often, they hadn't had any practice. It showed but they both laughed as the skaters fell on their rears.

CHAPTER VIII: THE DARKNESS DISAPPEARS

She was beginning to laugh, joke and take interest in the lives of others. Marsha called from Augusta; she and Wayne (smiley) were settled near the Medical College of Georgia, she had a job with MCG, as a patients' rep, looking into issues between the hospital and the patient. It was a 2year residency in Internal Medicine and they would be married then. Morgan wondered if they slept in separate beds but believed so.

Back at school, things were well; the students were attentive; the girls asking where she obtained her clothes as they were really into that now. It is true that Morgan could look fine in a burlap bag; it was rumored that she was known as the 'Fox" by the older boys. Why not? She was young, pretty, smart; what else could she do? Jump over a tall building, fly faster than a speeding bullet, you name it.

Dave was becoming familiar around her house; so easy to talk to and cooperative in everything. He was actually born in Sylvester, just down the road; but had been in Prosperity for 2-3 years. He did ask Morgan to his apartment; she found it to be pristine, clothing laid away and more than 2 coats. It was not large with one bedroom, sitting room, kitchen and 2 full baths. His linen closet was neater than Morgan's so she failed to comment beyond "you have a good maid, Dave". He "you're right, I am lucky in that and to be with you". He was so good about turning any remark into a compliment for Morgan; she appreciated his positive attitude.

In January 2000, they dated regularly as the bond grew stronger. Morgan thought "when two people of opposite sex are able to discuss in detail any subject without emotion, it's a fine situation". Her teaching was getting better as her experience level rose; Psychology was the most difficult to teach and the most challenging to the students. No wonder, studying the causes of human reactions to events is most tedious. Generally, Morgan and Dave went out at least twice a week as he came to the gym the nights that she was on duty. They kissed as most young adults do and, at times, she felt like more was needed. She never said anything to Dave but the steam did, at times, get up in her. "Yes" thought Morgan, men are likely to be more energetic but not for certain. She and Dave were at his apartment one evening sitting on the couch, listening to classical music. She leaned over and kissed him with an open mouth; he returned it as he shifted to be closer to her. Morgan turned into him so that her breast was on his chest. Whether he intended to touch it or not, his hand cupped her firm grapefruit. She asked" do you like it and would you like to kiss it?" Dave could hardly speak, he was so excited. Morgan removed her blouse and bra, revealing her beauties. Dave moved his mouth to one, taking it as a Hershey's Kiss, feeling her warmth and silky skin. Dave played with both of them as she kissed his face. After a few, Dave said "we need to stop now and cool down". Morgan nodded her head as he began to ease off. It was close but both were careful to be cautious.

Dave was so happy that she permitted him to take liberties with her breasts; he couldn't think of any other sexual act with her. She repaired her dress and he took her home; a kiss in the car and then into the house.

Morgan got a letter from Bud, the one with no stamp on it, just a writing by the serviceman of 'exempt' in the top right corner of the envelope. It was short, without details on combat or any gruesome events. It was just a little personal but primarily one friend corresponding to the other. She enjoyed it, planning to write him back; informing him of her current status, without names. She "Bud, I pray for you; it's not practical to tell you to be careful. Just do your job; we don't need any more heroes from that theatre".

Within the week, she wrote back to Bud. She informed Dave of the letters; another door closed, daylight was on the way. She and Dave had a mature relationship so revealing about one's personal life was normal. He didn't know Bud at all but did hear his name around town. School was almost through mid-March, time for a break. Dave wanted to take Morgan to the beach at Panama City or another on Florida's West coast. Panama City would likely be overflowing with the College and High School kids so they decided to try a beach to the East of the crowded beach in the Panhandle of Florida. Actually, she had 9 days but travel and prep for the last Quarter ate some of it. The amount of time set aside by the two was Saturday, after school let out, till the following Wednesday; the trip was about a half-day.

The beach was on the Gulf, beautiful white sand, with sea oats and sea grass in abundance. The quarters were about 50 yards from the beach, with two BRs, 11/2 baths, small kitchen and a sitting room in the middle. It was airconditioned but at night, it was off as the sea breezes flew through the open windows. Just down the street was a seafood restaurant called 'Blackbeard's'; it was in character, with sawdust on the floors and the waitresses wearing half blouses, cupped under their breasts. Not like Hooter's but not far from it. They tried it the first night; Morgan had a seafood latter with a bit of all types of sea characters. Dave liked the flounder so he dug in.

Very good. Naturally we walked around from our apartment to the restaurant from the house and back. We sat on our steps watching the boats lit up as they sailed across the Gulf. We'd had a busy day so we decided to turn in. Dave "which room do you want, Sweetheart?" Morgan, softly" the same one that you have, Darling" Both laughed. Morgan knew that the extra room was for her parents' benefit.

Dave was in bed first as Morgan did her usual at night: makeup, hair, clothing hung neatly, etc. She put on her short nightgown with nada underneath. She slid in the opposite side, touching Dave, He turned to her, gently kissed her as her gown rode up her body. As her twins met his chest, he hugged her, but gently, then Morgan took his hand placing it on her vagina, alive with a multitude of black hairs. Dave was speechless; she was naked and now was he. He had the proper item to insure safety so he put one on, with lubrication on the outside. He as on the right side of the bed, enabling his right arm to reach across, stroking her silk. She was as moist as a bath cloth, indicating an eagerness to meld.

The foreplay continued for a time as Morgan used her hands to discover all about Dave. It could not be restrained as one hot part met a volcano of desire. It began easily with both joining into this celebration of love. The tempo increased as these two became adjusted to each other's body. Time was unimportant in this initial coitus of Morgan and Dave. Dave indicated the plateau as he coughed once; she breathed deeply, mumbling " I'm ready". They managed the fireworks simultaneously; both falling back in the bed.

Lying there, just thinking; the vitality came back, letting them speak; Dave "Morgan, it reminded me of that beach scene in 'From Here To Eternity' with Kerr and Lancaster". Morgan "Maybe better, no sand or salty water". They laughed just before dozing off. They enjoyed the closeness as much, or more, than the physical portion of their joining.

In the AM, they walked to the restaurant where a buffet was set with sausage, grits, English muffins, OJ, ham, waffles, bacon, etc. A feast for hungry landlubbers; including Morgan and Dave. They ate on the deck, slowly and methodically; enjoying all the settings. Morgan "Dave, this is wonderful, the scenery, the climate, the crowd and the food. Who can want more?" Dave "Don't forget that trim brunette with the Colgate smile" Morgan smiled, acknowledging the compliment. Before returning to the cottage, they walked on the beach, finding starfish and shells and debris from the high tide.

They put on their suits, Morgan in a dainty 2 pieced yellow attire; Dave in the usual blue with the Dolphin affixed. She was a knockout with her selection, turning heads from 75 yards away. The tide was receding so swimming was out; there were lounge chairs so Dave appropriated two for their brief sunbathing. It was hot and getting hotter so 30 minutes was adequate at one time. They returned to the cottage to watch TV and talk. Changing back to land clothing, their interchanges were pleasant, each teasing the other about anything at all. It approached Noon and they sipped juice to hold down any dehydration.

There was news from the Middle East, no units were named but that area was where Bud was last stationed. Morgan didn't want to borrow trouble but was concerned.

CHAPTER IX:
RIDING THE WAVE

The trip was wonderful, she and Dave had grown together; she knew that he was a man not a wannabe; he could think and analyze for himself; not taking a poll of friends. In fact, she concluded, ones like Dave and herself, did not have loads of friends; in fact, no one did really; they might have acquaintances but if seriously connected, there was not much time for others. The final day, they ate in the AM at the restaurant, hating to leave but wanting to find out the news around Prosperity. It had a weekly newspaper that did print national and foreign events, but by then, we had learned from TV and big newspapers the sense of the event.

Dave dropped me and I got to work right then; my dirty clothes sandy shoes and wrinkled shorts and blouses, made me nervous. Morgan mused 'you know, this girl has always been particular about her 'threads' and this habit is eternal. Morgan "I believe that guys like this habit; it indicates discipline; so, I'll keep on doing it". Her Mom noticed her cheerfulness, remarking "Morgan you'll wash those clothes apart if you don't ease up". Morgan "Ok Mom, I 'm just excited about everything, forgive me". She continued her work. She daydreamed as she toiled, just viewing her and Dave as a couple.

School started back for the last Quarter of the year; this would complete her first year as a teacher; she felt as if she had taught for a longer period. What would she do this Summer? That was a thought; the Principal had offered her the job of tutoring the laggards if she wanted. Morgan was unsure if she wanted to be tied down but spending 11 weeks around here unoccupied was not inviting. There was always Mercer to work on her Masters. Hmmm, that's a thought. But what about Dave? She would likely have to get an apartment or better, stay in the dorm. Like Scarlett, she'd decide that tomorrow.[1]

She had the other Senior class this Quarter; so it would require more memory of names; all classes had one or more who were out of their depth; they had been promoted primarily to move them along, on out of school. A few had real learning problems and some were just stubborn and defiant. Their families, in many cases, were not interested in education, as they were farmers and only interested in their boys' learning the agricultural mores. Not great attitudes but Morgan thought that she could cope with them. She would move them along, also, and keep them from disrupting the class. Morgan retrieved her Psychology books from Mercer, determined to delve into the psyches of those who were unready.

Calling the roll, the first day, she said 'Bud Southerland' and no response; then she saw a hand raised in the back of the classroom. Morgan said "are you Bud?" He responded "yeah". She "you know that you should answer when your name is called?" Bud "OK" She left it there; he could be difficult or just showing off; he could not stay in Psychology, it was too difficult. Maybe, the 'Shop' class had an opening? She got through the entire class, without mispronouncing a single name; not an easy task when many names had been handed down, often losing a letter in the process. Often, they had only letters:

1 :Gone With The Wind by Margaret Mitchell, 1933

J D, O C, N B but the girls had double names, Mary Jo, Rose Mary, Betty Sue; you get it.

Now that they knew each other, or thought that they did; it was time to assign a bit of homework; just 6 pages in the U.S. History book. Morgan thought that was reasonable but was about to learn about their abilities. They were in other classes so she had them for Homeroom and History. Morgan felt that some had already done some 'digging' into her past life from the way they, or some, stared at her. Maybe, it was her clothes; the teachers here, much older, were not attired in the trendy fashions.

The faculty meetings and duties took up the slack in the days; when school was out, not only the students, but the keepers of the institution, were ready to be released. Of course, 'bus duty was the pits, seeing that all got on the right bus, without tearing each other apart over some trivial misunderstanding. She noticed Bud, large for his age, right in the center of any conflict. For them, talking was over when the bell rang; it was time for Mr. Fist to enter the ring. Often, someone got on the bus, blood running down his face; defiantly threatening to 'get' the other the next day. And did.

Morgan didn't forget Dave, calling him to invite him to dinner with the family; he accepted arriving at 6:30P. Morgan and her guest sat in the swing on the back porch, exchanging thoughts about everything. They wanted to go out later but said nothing out loud. There was a movie (comedy) named "The 7 Year Itch", with Tom Ewell and Marilyn Monroe; Bud with his humor, referred to unwed couples as, The7 Day Itch, implying that their testosterone exceeded normal levels. Morgan agreed, all in good fun.

Between teaching and the family and Dave, Morgan was occupied. Bud, she heard, had returned to Macon but still subject to recall if the unit had a deployment. The door closed on that chapter. She and Dave, 6 feet, 175, soft brown hair, hazel eyes and a sense of humor; were a larger item, almost as if they were handcuffed to one another. Not much travelling as the hot weather inhibited almost any physical activity. Even hanky-panky, thought Morgan, necessitated air conditioning turned up high. Two in love could always find a way and route to get 'there'. She was always asked about 'marriage' and she replied "Yes, I'm old enough, 26, but haven't asked Dave yet".

Keeping it light was the preferable way to proceed. She and Dave had discussed it but she needed to earn her Master's Degree before 'settling down'. She was planning in a week or so to go to Valdosta State College, on I-75 to enroll. It would take 2 Summers but by 2003, she'd have it. Not an economic wizard but, she knew that the pay jumped quite a bit for the MED. Dave supported her in this move.

She had discussed with her Dad about buying a home, in the edge of Prosperity; she needed her own space and so did they, not having to worry about a 26year old daughter staying ou late. Her Dad located one as requested on the outskirts of town, frame, 2 BRS, 11/2 baths, sitting room and kitchen, with a large lot, and no near neighbors. She had some money and her Dad helped with the down payment; she was now a property owner.

The house did have a carport; Morgan hated garages where someone could hem you up in the dark. As most ladies can imagine an intruder hiding in the shadows, Morgan had that concern. Dave helped her move her possessions, little besides clothing and shoes; the furniture would be accumulated bit by bit, from consignment sales, gifts and estates. Finally, her goods were all 'aboard' and she invited Dave over for the initial dinner; Morgan was scared to death about cooking; it had been awhile since she had worn an apron. Hmmm. Let's see; what is easier to prepare? She reached the conclusion that a steak, salad and potato were the simplest of all to prepare. Voila'.

Dave came with vino and flowers and a clock-radio; no more rushing for Morgan. They acted like two kids, and, why not; love is the commodity that is not for sale. They nibbled at the food, both looking at each other; Dave cleaned the dishes away. The lights were low as they sat on the couch presented by the faculty. The music was soft with Dean Martin in his best form. Morgan kissed Dave and he held her loosely; her firm breast resting on her arm. Shifting, he cupped it as she began to breathe more rapidly. Morgan "I forgot something in the BR, can you help me find it?" Dave, alert, said "Madam, I am at your disposal".

The rest of the evening was unknown as Morgan pulled the shades (old fashioned, on a roller). It was hers, all her own, and she was proud of it; her hard work was paying off. On Monday, she enrolled at VSC, beginning her trek to the Master's; there was a carpool, not every day, but Monday and Friday; the real work was done out of class as their papers on a variety of subjects were developed. The course ended just before the Georgia schools began. Morgan shifted gears from student to teacher, still with the Juniors and Seniors. The new classes were not noteworthy except that a majority were female, a mixture of 'town' girls and rural ones; not a problem by itself, but could be touchy as they, when asked to talk briefly about themselves, often both groups embellished their resume's. Not unusual but a bit much at their ages, 17-18.

Maybe just the nervousness of the new year, but Morgan wanted to stop any division of the class as it could fraction it, inhibiting her efforts at cooperation. But, a crisis at this time was likely only one of several; Morgan was concerned about the 'whole banana', the future of these classes and these kids. While it was true that there were no jobs for these students, either now after school or after graduation. Almost all left, for college, the services or seminaries. The few left married or worked on their relative's farm. Most never returned to Prosperity except for one brief minute, just to see if it was still the same. It was.

Morgan knew that it was impossible to create new opportunities but still lamented the loss of these young talents. Moving on, football was in the air and Morgan was selling tickets at the game; suddenly she looked up from the tickets AND Bud was there, leering, his normal gaze. "Hi, Teach, how's the High School?" M "just great, Bud, you look well". B "that farm work keeps one slimmed down; you look good, Miss Morris". M "thank you Bud; you work with your Father?" Bud "Nah, my Uncle, ole Dad and I don't Gee-Hah"[2]. He moved on. Morgan knew that these were the most words that she had ever heard from him; was he growing up?"

She often saw her former students but few disturbed her like Bud; he seemed probing; maybe he had a running mate, to teach him more meanness. He had enough scrapes in high school to give him experience for life. She thought, 'if he stays on the farm, avoiding alcohol, he might have a reasonable life'.

The others that ran across Morgans path were polite, friendly and open about their lives. The girls, now Mothers, were taking care of small ones, helping their mostly farmer husbands, going to church and being good citizens. Morgan took pride in her students, even Bud, the farmer, whose mental makeup did not equip him for much in life.

This year was almost over as most students did very well. It was strange but it seemed that a number of the town girls had gravitated towards the farm boys as a few of the rural girls had been going with the city lads. Most of these were married that Summer and most remained so. Morgan was back to VSC for her final session. The same routine as before, to and back from Valdosta. Morgan knew the drill on the homework; her knowledge of computers and wordsmithing greatly assisted her. Before the peanuts were ready, she had her degree, desired by all teachers; placing her on a pedestal, similar to the trophies that she had one. Graduation Day, Dave drove Morgan; afterwards the two had lunch and she went shopping for a few clothes for school. Back to Prosperity, Dave thought that they needed to get 'together' tonight so they stopped at his apartment. Morgan had not time during the Summer

2 An old saying when mules were in vogue meaning 'right,left'

to spend many evenings alone with Dave, so, this was a treat for her. Dave cracked a bottle of wine; Morgan sipped a little as they got closer to the bedroom. It was better than ever; Morgan was not cold or even cool; she could be warm to warmer to hot. Dave knew the keys to getting her motor running and delighted in pushing the buttons.

Another year with new students, new attitudes and new energy; Morgan was in a great mood to move through this year, 2003, excelling in teaching with a new pay scale, assisting her in saving for her marriage, when it arrived. The initial meeting between the class and Morgan was friendly and open; they knew of Morgan's achievements, I.e. the beauty contests, the Master's and just her great looks and personality. For the first time, she selected two students, one male and one female, to assist her in grading tests and other class duties. She chose the best and the brightest.

Her classes were interesting and informative but she felt something missing; she had an offer for two afternoons and nights weekly by the Worth Community College, in Sylvester, Georgia, 20 miles away; to teach Psychology and Sociology to adults. Many from local law enforcement agencies flocked to sign up for her courses. It was a load but she was very fit and already knew her subjects. Dave wasn't sure but she calmed him with "darling, this can help us reach our goal for the marriage". Who could resist that?

Most of her Psychology class were deputies, policemen, DEA personnel and GBI men; divided into two sizes, ones hanging over their belts and the leaner, whose belts were in the 5th hole or more. They were all friendly, eager to learn primarily about judging suspects in any crime; what to look for, how to observe them, their mannerisms and all about ones who might be involved in criminality. Looks were not it solely; the question was "how does a criminal look?" Answer "look in the mirror". Morgan thought "we always see the worst type of suspect but the crime is the indicator" Common law offenses usually bring the lowest of mankind as they seek instant money. White collar crimes and even murder up the looks, at least, of suspects.

The classes were 3 hours each with one break in which Morgan was bombarded with questions by her students. She managed to hold most of these for the class to educate the entire class. As one might guess, most f the class involved cases or instances of illegal behavior; from completely insane down to the lower degrees of misbehavior, involving limited intelligence and bi-polar, not recognized in most states as a mental illness.

Morgan normally left for the short ride at 2P, starting at 3:30P till 6:30. Dave drove her often and they would eat in Sylvester afterwards. She was a celebrity among law enforcement, all paying her homage for her skills. As among all groups, there were a few younger troopers, anxious to earn their spurs by nabbing a high-profile offender or perp. These kidded with her more as they were similar in age.

As Morgan balanced her responsibilities as a waiter in a 'gin' house, her mind was always engaged. From graduating students to those performing the most dangerous tasks; all needed assistance and her performance was critical to the pyramid. She began to recognize their names, even though she did not call the roll; either they were there or they were not. Often some were absent on a mission and she did give a bit of 'makeup' to these. Once every two weeks, she asked for a 2page paper on a certain problem; this was required just to ascertain if they were up with the course. Moreover, she wanted to learn how effectively they wrote. She knew that the proper use of grammar could give the author's correct analysis of the matter, as the placement of a comma in the wrong area could skew the intent of the writer.

Morgan viewed the WCC classes as icing on the cake and the high school duties as the substance of her efforts. Financially, she was saving money, thanks to Dave's driving and feeding her. She was fortunate to always have friends like him. It was another Holiday Season, another break and more presents, down to 3 from her. Out on the 17th, later this year than usual; she talked Dave into shopping one class day in Sylvester; for a 'farm' town' it was shaping up, adding a Walmart, a CVS and two apparel/variety shops. One was a men's clothing and accessory retail establishment with some trendy duds. She sent Dave to the CVS as she bought him a raincoat/overcoat; her budget was bent but he merited it. Her Dad got a spiffy apron for his dishwashing chores; Mom a new purse to replace her Vietnam era, almost Alligator, relic. All done, thought Morgan, and not too much pain. They departed, Dave stopped at a large Oak adjacent to the roadway, with the limbs hanging almost to the ground.

Morgan thought 'what's he doing ?'He drove behind the tree to avoid eyes. Dave "I've always wanted to kiss you in the 'open' spaces but safety demanded restraint. Now if we can have a kiss to remember, we can go on". She laughed, kissing him with a full dose of her holiday lipstick. Dave said "yum, yum". Back home.

The night before, they exchanged presents; hers, a sporty hat, riding breeches and everyday boots. Actually, Morgan's wardrobe had worn with the constant activity of classes; everything was her need. Dave and she enjoyed their respites from the daily drudgeries of repetitive work.

Back to School was actually welcomed after a number of indolent days; the kids had presents to show off, including an engagement ring or two, with minuscule diamonds, not to be mentioned. Some of the boys received hunting rifles or shotguns for quail, rabbits or doves. Don't forget those fast greenheads.

Basketball was in; normally the rural schools could put up a fine BB team, girls or boys; however, this year, the old saying was back "we're not very big but we're slow". Nothing left to say. Morgan's duties were small due to her second job so she was not out at night often. She visited her family at least twice a week and she and Dave were together at least 3 afternoons/nights. She had two nights to read or brush up on the latest findings on Psychology. More articles reflecting the author's opinions, not certified, were emerging, including the multiple persons occupying certain patients. The "Three Faces of Eve" written by a N. Augusta S.C. Psychiatrist,[3] a movie also, was the first actual documentation of this theory. Now accepted by the medical profession as more than a theory; as a medical fact.

The school year was concluding; high school was ending, but the WCC job was continuing, thank goodness. She looked in the mirror, saw a beautiful young lady with no wrinkles but was uneasy about her future. Why hadn't they married; where was her ring? She called Dave "Dave, were going for my ring tonight; we love each other and my third finger needs cover. Pick me up now". Dave "I'm underway now." In 6 minutes, he pulled up "darling, what's up; you could have that ring any time". M "I want it now".

There was no place in our town to buy a fashionable ring so on to Tifton; they had at least four jewelry stores. They started at the best store, as they understood it. It wasn't the price solely, but Morgan wanted a statement. They brought out 'baby rays' very tiny diamonds, an insult. Dave "don't you have any genuine engagement rings?". The clerk swallowed his mustache as he gulped "yes Sir". He then brought out $3500-5000 stones that one could actually see; there was a $4500 one with a platinum setting; 5 stones of .40 carets each, 2 carets total. Morgan tried it on; it fit; Dave pulled out his credit cards, made the transaction, Morgan wore it home. There was only one celebration left and Morgan needed it.

As she taught in the summer, the ring on Morgan's finger insured that all knew her status; no one would approach her about anything except classwork. Dave seemed to be more relaxed with the crisis resolved. The summer zipped by; they took in 3 days on the West coast of Florida at the beach. Great to get away, thought Morgan.

3 DR.Thigpen; a large brouhah arose among the professionals as to the validity of this finding.

Another Senior class; all of them were different; but all looking for the Holy Grail of Diplomas. If Morgan had her way, they'd get them. Now and then, Morgan ran into one of her students, usually married and looking perhaps more elderly than herself; Marriage in these parts, especially the farming centers, was not easy; Love was one thing, surmised Morgan; but the trials of farm life with its dry wells, dead livestock, droughts, lack of help and, above all, the eroding away of a couple by debt. These were just the beginning of a lengthy list of draining issues, requiring the wives to be on the forefront with the Spouse. A 25yearold woman could pass for 10 or more years older; as this occurred, her smile receded into the realities of being a farmer's wife without a family to pitch in. In farming, experience is valuable but the best can be ground up by the fortunes of the dirt farmer. Not as bad as the 1930s'The Grapes Of Wrath', but when the four men of the Apocalypse, or even one rides over a tiller of the soil, he is crushed.

Morgan hated to see one as described but it is life even if it seems like death. She was practical as others, understanding the necessity for a steady occupation not destroyed by the changes of the economy, the weather or the health of the breadwinner. The Vietnamese Conflict, some 25 years in the rear mirror brought out the best and the worst in Americans. For the enlisted men who served willingly in support of their leaders, even though they were wrong, there is admiration. For some others who dodged the draft, perhaps disqualified, who took the jobs of those who took the rifles, we must question some of their morals, integrity and bravery. Some of these might just be fortunate but for the ones, not a few, who were manipulative, we should avoid any admiration. The other side of the coin is that many of the latter are embarrassed when the Vets are in the crowd. There is a deep silence so their dues are being paid.

Morgan thought of her friend, Bud and his acceptance of his birthright of patriotism and fealty, without cajoling him to go to the deserts of death. She was thankful that he returned a whole man, in mind and body. Enough of the morbid, thought Morgan.

Another Winter for Morgan with her two groups of students; one at least 20 years older than the other. Neither group was great at homework but their classroom attention was very good. Soon it was the Spring break; a few of the kids who had some money went to Lauderdale and a few went to the lake outside Cordele; was it Blackshear? All parents were happy when their offspring remained near home; a lot less peer pressure to act out of the ordinary. When they began the Spring Quarter, most started planning their colleges, the military services, a few jobs or travel to the Continent.

June 2003 was here; graduation, marriages, enlistees shipping out and the wrap of the year by post-planning. Morgan was not into this but had to go with the flow; it, like everything, would pass. She and Dave decided to go to the mountains in North Carolina, the Smokies, by travelling through Western Carolina, spending a night here and another in a new village. The trip was ten days and the travel was enough for each of them.

Morgan and Dave had been so wrapped up in themselves and their duties that they had lost contact with the 30yearold crowd in Prosperity; the precise folks that both needed for a real social life. The group AKA the Comers were having a party just to rejuvenate their activities; it was at a barn on a few acres of a member. Morgan and Dave jumped at the invite; this was for them. On a Thursday night, Dave and Morgan, dressed casually, swung by the barn. A number of cars were there so they went in. They were met by the sponsors, introduced and then met the others; a number had not arrived. The married and single were about 50-50, the singles being younger. In fact, Morgan spied one or two of her former pupils; she waved at them. Apparently, it was to be light refreshments, dancing with maybe a square dance or two; the object was to introduce all the younger people to the others SO when an event was planned, they could have a nice turnout; it was working.

Many knew Morgan from her contests and teaching at WCC but Dave was relatively unknown, as he was not a Prosperity native. Everyone was friendly, inquiring this and that and trying to keep everyone straight. The leader made a short welcome to the crowd; there was a local band playing soft rock, R and B, and some C and W. She and Dave nibbled at the snacks, talked to many, most of whom wanted to know when the event would be. Marriage of course. We dodged it be saying that Dave was under consideration as an engineer on the large nuclear plant in Burke County (Waynesboro). The selection time was unknown; only a white lie; Morgan avoided the black ones. Dave later laughed about it.

They tried a square dance, avoiding getting anyone hurt, laughing about their moves. She and Dave danced a couple of ballroom dances and did a 'shag' where you swing her out, and then turn her around as you rotated yourself. Naturally, Morgan was on her game but did her best to make Dave look good as well. The affair was well done; Morgan gave her cell number to several in order to be contacted for future events; she said that she would notify Dave. It wound up around 10P and Dave stayed awhile at Morgan's place, leaving before too late. At times, Morgan couldn't get enough of Dave, maybe it was her womanly hormones; whatever, she did care for that man. His kiss was so gentle, sincere and exciting that she could kiss hi0 all night long. Since there were neighbors not too far away, Dave didn't stay overnight; not in Prosperity.

The Summer of 2003 was by before anyone knew it; school was starting, classes at the high school and the CC began almost at the same time. New students at PHS but mostly the same at the Community College. Morgan was to teach Intermediate Psychology to the government employees; the ones who had credit for the first course. This course went deeper into the traits, attitudes, schemes, devices and propensities of the more severely mentally impaired criminals. These thoughts were very helpful in evaluating impaired persons to determine IF this one was likely to commit the act in question. The investigators really enjoyed the details of this course; to see some taking notes was gratifying to Morgan. She, like all, needed some positive results from her efforts and DID get them from these guys.

Fall Quarter was very different from the other seasonal periods; football was in but the quality of the team was unknown; it seemed that the team usually relied on, almost totally, on Juniors and Seniors, leaving the team the next year with only experienced rising Seniors, put the team back in the same spot; seasoned Seniors BUT green underclassmen who were in their 4th-5th game before jelling. However, the local crowd wanted to watch who ever played; regardless of skills. Again, Morgan was working at the game, but no surprises this time.

When one is enjoying their work and personal life, it is similar to the Willard Klutchmeyer look of the 60s, in Mad Magazine, with the toothy smile and curly locks, saying "what, Me worry?" But, to ride the crest of a slippery dagger, holding on with a mayonnaise glove can be unsettling. As the world turns, so do our fortunes; Morgan and many viewed setbacks as bad luck, ill fortune or their unfortunate birth date; but bad luck as the term goes, might just be the result of bad decision making. As Jimmy the Greek opined: you might beat the odds at times, but the odds are set for reasons, not merely to balance the betting.

Morgan was at her house just beginning the 'break', trying to put up a tree and decorate it; the chair in which she stood was not overly steady. The reach to install the star was the Humpty Dumpty event of the day; Morgan fell, not breaking a bone, but spraining her ankle, requiring crutches for a time. This injury was 'bad luck' or was the chair faulty or the tree too tall or Morgan was too tired or the decision was flawed? Only choose all. Morgan called Dave as she wrapped her ankle with the 'Ace' bandage; aware immediately of the specific injury.

Crutches in hand, Morgan did her holiday shopping as all carried her possessions to her car. Dave said "Morgan, if we'd been married, you wouldn't be on crutches; it would be me". Moran laughed at Dave and his straight face. But will wins out and she made it through the holiday period. One New Year's Resolution was to purchase a decorated tree in 2005. The usual presents for her Mom and Dad but Dave? Morgan thought of wrapping her body in Christmas paper and a red bow, giving herself to him; she knew he'd be ecstatic with that gift but; practicality swept the day with a foot warmer for those weary days.

Prosperity did have a new high-toned variety store with gifts for this season so let's try it. Morgan with her crutches was a frequent sight around town; every male jumped to assist her; at school those rough boys softened to be the men that she had expected. They vied to carry her books or personal items; the courtesies shown "Miss Morgan' were heartwarming to their parents and their teacher.

School must go on with the Winter quarter in session; she could not stand so the boys rigged up another chair with pillow for her sore ankle. Her mind was on their welfare as she taught like never before; using patience with all and never neglecting to compliment better performances.

Morgan's social life was curtailed during this period; she and Dave settled in to dinner, brought in, a quiet time afterwards to discuss national and local news; just valuable exchanges between friends/lovers. At the correct time, Dave kissed her and said 'goodnight', my love. This was one of Morgan's memorable times, recuperating from her injury. It took more than a sprain to keep this lady out of the mainstream.

Morgan also appreciated her students' extra efforts at learning the materials presented by her; her vocal responses by each indicated their concentration on the subject matters, critical to the diploma at the conclusion of the year. Her two student helpers did well in their efforts to maintain consistency in the classroom.

Morgan and Dave got back into the socializing of the young people, attending a wild game dinner at a Lodge owned by parents of one; a few guys had over a month or so, taken a multitude of wild game, primarily those with wings and feathers. The quail, doves, duck and one deer, were the mix; now was needed one to be the chef; to cook without extremes, retaining the moisture within the meat. Most had not eaten ever, or lately, this type of repast, so there was a large turnout for the event. The ladies were timid because of the word "wild", giving them an idea of some shack in the wilderness, with its bearded occupant using rocks to subdue the small birds.

Morgan didn't exactly 'dig in' the feast but snacked around the edges, and, to her surprise, had a taste for the menu items. She found these birds sweet and succulent; a menu for anyone. While dining, the two went around speaking to most; it had been some time since they had been together. There was generally no alcohol at these functions, but this night, the two glass/beer rule was in effect; no more than 2 moderate wine/beer glasses. Morgan liked that; she had avoided since an early age, alcohol and those who imbibed. It was not a religious decision but was a decision based on observing others.

Morgan had school duties, despite her injury but did these with efficiency; working the ticket booth and snack stand, while sitting on a stool. It gave her a chance to see and meet those related or connected to the students; something rarely done. She was better and the Doctor was going to a 'boot' with her; not attractive but functional; goodbye crutches.

Winter quarter was closing, tests were completed, and in accordance with her procedures, all students passed, some with a bit of help. These young people would one day; some of them, would be the leaders of this area or the state. They HAD to get out of school to try their wings so some help was in order. The Spring break came as usual; some students as before going to Florida beaches, but not Lauderdale, once there was enough, massive crowds, no housing, no space, nothing but young people looking for 'the action'

Morgan and Dave might return to Florida or try the South Carolina coast, with Hilton Head, Edisto, Pawley's Island; a bit farther but less congestion and housing reasonably available.

CHAPTER X:
LIFE AS IT WAS

The two riding up I 95 from Savannah, Georgia just checking out the coast for a nice beach and housing other than motels; Hilton Head was too trendy, there was a beach at Beaufort on a small island, but it was unknown. On up the coast to a sign pointing to Edisto Island/Beach, 20 miles off the mainland, but good roads. A family place, but hospitable, stated the service station attendant. They agreed to go turning off I 95.

The trip from I-95 to Edisto Island was uneventful, the marshes and sea grass were on both sides of the 2 lane, paved road. Before reaching the beach area, Morgan, the sightseer, noticed a few shops on the right and some native, grassed sales outlets, on the left. These were small for 1 or 2 persons to sell their crabs, fish, fish bait, fresh vegetables; usually with the first name of the owner affixed. Along with the name was a caution "nuttin lagee den a 20". Well said; they were born here as were their parents; a large plantation was here until 1865, when there was no money or labor to operate it. It was divided into 40acre tracts and given to former slaves to farm. They were required (or told) to live on the land, pay the taxes and be the owner after 3 years. This sounded fair but for folks with no money, equipment, mules or supplies; it seemed like a long rocky road on bare feet. Moreover, many had begun or were into fishing and the conditions did not suit their fancies. Almost half of the blacks on the Island had never farmed; some had been 'freedmen' moving down from Charleston as they were not suited as 'house' servants OR did not like the dipping and bowing. Farming was not god on Edisto as the grantees failed to pay taxes or legally transfer the property to another,

Later, talking to a couple of elderly descendants of the slaves, we learned that a name for these matters was 'heirs' property', as in most cases, there was no administration of estates or wills; pages numbered when the alleged owner died, nothing except the burial was done. The oldest child of the decedent at home took charge and generations following had a right w/o a title.

As Morgan and Dave entered the beach area, the blue sea caught their eyes; few on the beach; stopping at the grocery and inquiring about quarters or a room; the Fairfield, home of the only golf course, rented condos and cottages were for rent. The less expensive ware the condos, and the most modern; Fairfield was within walking distance of the beach with a restaurant. They could drive to the beach if they did not block a pathway.

Checking into the Fairfield, they were on 2d floor, with a great view of the beach and bay. They suited up, grabbed the sun screen, and towels; driving the 1/8mile, parking NOT on the pathways. It didn't take long for Mr. Sol to tingle their skins, giving fair warning that this is his place. After the journey, they felt a bit weary so they got a couple of sodas and sandwiches, settling in the room. There was no boardwalk and only one spot near the pier with a juke box; the teens flocked there.

The waiter said that one boat carried passengers, for a half day, out to the deep water, where the bottom fishing (150 ft) was good;

the red snapper were plentiful. He said that if either Morgan or Dave wanted, he would call the owner and arrange it. Morgan "Dave, I might just drive around the area, you go". Dave "You'll be OK? It's something that I've never done and this is my chance. I'll be back by 12:30, Sweetie".

The trip was on; Morgan dropped him at the pier at 7A with his sun screen, glasses and hat as well as a small ice chest with water, soda and a snack. The boat had several already aboard, and looked if it could accommodate 8-10 fishermen. Morgan left, just driving around, she couldn't get lost, she hoped. She wanted to see the farmland and did; it was not as she expected, deep, black, loam soil, not here. She kept driving past the huts of the real natives, no pretense, all worked at something. She did speak to one or two, but couldn't understand them. She stopped at a store, talked to an employee who said "that's Gullah, their language from Africa, perhaps modified a bit but still difficult for us to understand; I do understand enough to get by but if you hear two or more talking, good luck" Morgan thought 'not being very good at languages, I'll skip the Gullah'.

Dave arrived back at the pier at 12:45 with 2 large red snapper ; Morgan and he returned to Fairfield, where Dave requested the Chef, asking if he could prepare the fish for tonight. It was a 10-4 so that was taken care of. Morgan and Dave met a couple from Dublin, another large farming county; Jim and Edith Lovett, owners of a mill and gin there. This county, Laurens, was on the Oconee River, composed of numbers of agricultural support businesses, to include tractor and farm implement operations, silos and railroads to insure the swift movements of crops, finished products and equipment from the factories thru Dublin to the farms. Just one vast conglomerate delivering food and fiber to the entire East Coast as well as overseas.

It was nice, Morgan thought, to be with some fellow Georgians who were out seeking new places and ideas. At dinner, Jim brought 2 bottles of white wine, Cabernet Sauvignon, to wash our dusty throats. So much talking and laughing among us that we took our time eating. Wow, in our little part of the world, fish meant red breast bream, catfish or trout. Fresh water was limited on its ability to produce and maintain many species of fish. After dining, the four went into the lounge to listen to the guitar player, who could play and sing as Johnny Cash, gave us goose bumps with is rendition of RING OF FIRE. He mellowed it down soon into a Charley Pride number, HE STOPPED LOVING HER TODAY, about a lady's suitor, unsuccessful, who had died.

We had a cordial in the bar, full of ice; Morgan joined us, a bit unusual for her but the mood was festive. After this day, all were weary and said goodnight, going to their condos. Sleep came easy and the dreams also; Morgan awoke first at 8A, not waking Dave as she retrieved coffee, and sat on the little outside porch. She watched the fishing boats as they disappeared over the horizon; Dave woke as she brought his coffee to him. Not much talking, just staring at the panorama of colors.

CHAPTER XI:
THE GOOD LIFE

They decided to go crabbing so retrieved a couple of chicken necks from the kitchen, bought a handled net and string; ready for the blue crabs, usually only caught on an incoming tide. The man said "don't let them die on you before cooking; keep them in water if you can. So, our two budding salt water experts were headed for the dock where the river joins the Atlantic. Dave fixed up a string line with a smaller string to tie the neck on. Then, the procedure is just let it down from the dock until it hits the bottom. Leave it 5-10 minutes, pull it up a bit to see if one was on; if so, ease it up to the net. If too small, leave him for another day. Dave and Morgan followed the procedures and within an hour, they had 8-10 large blue crabs. Time to go.

The crabs went directly to the kitchen for lunch to day. Then they decided to take a ride around the closer part of the Island, where the natives lived. The houses were little, all frame, each with its small garden adjacent to the house, usually a couple of rows of sugar cane for syrup or chewing. The roads were dirt for the most part, but passable, one car at a time. A little white washed church in the middle of the houses, usually listed AME Baptist or another denomination. It was nice to see this little village, where all owned their houses subject to a faulty title.

Back at the beach and Fairfield, the two checked in for lunch. The Chef had severed the claws, then cut the crab straight the shell, removing all except the white meat, placing these portions on a platter with slaw, having a small crusher for cracking the shells to remove the meat. It takes some effort to obtain enough meat to satisfy a man but practice makes perfect. Dave and Morgan were ready for this illusive meat, to be eaten with crackers, hot sauce, wine vinegar or any salad. They cleaned their plates.

Back in the room, they just lazed around, watching the news on TV. They discussed what they would do the next day; Dave "we can run into Charleston; it's only an hour". M "we could, maybe do some sightseeing,I.e. Fort Sumter, the Citadel, Battery Wagner on James Island (the remains of it), two old Episcopal Churches, downtown, a statue of John C Calhoun, famous Congressman from S. Carolina and more." Dave "all that in one day?" M "No, a half day". They both laughed.

Dave "let's go". She grabbed a hat and purse and they were off the beach area, onto the Island. The day was nice as they rode along towards Highway 17, the route to Charleston, some 25 miles away. Reaching there by 8:30, they drove to the battery from a tourist map. From there, they could view Ft. Sumter, in the center of the harbor, reconstructed to some degree but not to its original design. They were near St. Phillips and St. Wight, so rode by them, not entering. They took in the Market, in the near area with its seagrass baskets made by hand by the locals, other handmade goods as well as souvenirs of all types.

Riding in Charleston is not any delight with its narrow streets, lack of parking spaces and vast numbers of vehicles. Dave "we've seen it, should we find our way back or do you have an idea?" M "we can go if we can get out of this area; I'm ready". They found Highway 17 and remained on it until the turnoff to Edisto. Back at Fairfield, they had a light lunch; then back to the room for a rest before the afternoon. They would be leaving tomorrow so this would be their last meal here.

In the dining room, the waiter suggested the seafood platter, a mixture of local seafood on a platter garnished with a small baked potato and a fresh tomato. Both ordered the platters, trying a shrimp cocktail first. Great dining, Dave said" I can do this every week". Morgan" and they say that seafood is nonfattening". Dave" that's if you just taste it". The next morning, they were on the road by 8A, from Edisto to US 17 S, on to Beaufort to I 95, Savannah, I 16 to Dublin, then across to I 75 down to Ashburn, then to Prosperity, sounds confusing, but the State of Georgia is the largest state East of the Mississippi, with very few E-W highways.

Pulling in after 2P, both were tired; Morgan was dropped off as Dave returned to his apartment to recuperate from the trek. In 2 days, both had to go back to work; the following day was for recovering. She and Dave conversed by phone without any personal contact; both had lots of dirty clothes and the car must be cleaned to minimize the damage from the salt air.

School began for the final quarter of this academic year; Morgan knew her students at the high school very well and thought that almost all of them would do their best.

It was relatively easy for Morgan to shift gears from pleasure to work, as she did every year; good judgement was said to come experience that came from bad judgement. She was a seasoned professional now; able to have greater influences on the students than when she had doubts about herself. AS a teacher, it was necessary that she be also a Psychologist, a student of the mores and folkways of South Georgia, as well as a student of the Bible, especially the portions dealing with patience, kindness and faith.

All returned to class relating their experiences during the 'break'; Morgan noted a couple who said nothing about those few days; she knew the reason; their families were having tough financial times with an absence of money to spend on trivialities. She omitted any knowledge of this difficulty, acting as if she was unaware. So was the class and that was good. Morgan thought "this is an issue that is so tenuous and sensitive, that it's better left alone. The last thing that these youngsters needed; to be reminded of their poverty'.

Getting into the swing of it, Morgan began a few short oral exams; advising that if one had not read the material; then say 'unprepared' to bog down the class with lengthy excuses or a faulty recitation. This went well, assisting them in improving their speech abilities, as they gained confidence. New teaching procedures always worked for a while, then perhaps they lost their novelty and must be sidelined. Was Morgan becoming a philosopher as Cicero, or getting more experience?

Spring was lovely in Worth County, with the greenery spouting from the sandy loam soil; giving a feeling of life, hope and prosperity. Just riding through this large food- producing jurisdiction, was stimulating, educational and memorial. When one understood the relationship between the farmer on the dusty, loud tractor and the elite in New York enjoying his filet, without the perspiration that goes with its production. Those who labor in the sod understand their mission; so, does their family. It takes some of the city people longer to grasp the train of sustenance.

At the WCC, Morgan thought that a couple of the young rooster 'badges' at school were a bit too friendly towards her; feeling their oats towards all pretty ladies. She kept them in line at school; not socializing with them outside the confines of the schoolhouse. Morgan knew "that these few would calm down in time but respected herself more than to mingle with the troops". This was like a hangnail but still was a consideration for their senior.

She enjoyed these classes, at times, by presenting an 'issue' or real problem with misnamed individuals, perplexed by mental issues beyond their control. First, I asked one to identify the handicap; another to produce a solution and another to try to present a protection against being besieged by this defect. They, the protectors of the populace, benefitted from these 'drills' and, perhaps, used these to psychoanalyze their subjects, involved in various misconduct.

Morgan rarely gave them 'homework' as they were very busy and; could learn more than most by listening in class. She could say that she was friends with these saviors of the innocent. Her classes did change students as they rotated in and out; coming from surrounding areas, the class was varied as to responsibilities.

Spring was slipping by; it was difficult to keep my students in high school, alert with their eyes on the ball; focused on the finals and graduation. Morgan thinking "to think that I will never see again some of these students after the final day is depressing; but this is life and their destinies were determined some time ago, by their ancestors and their mores. To lead oneself into a morass of regret for things not correctible, is fruitless and unnecessary.

Morgan and Dave spent more time together during April and May 2003 than they had lately, minus the Edisto visit. It was not all dining out or attending 'young adults' socials. Many afternoons and nights they spent, with her studying for her classes as he worked on his stock portfolio or studied advanced authorities on nuclear energy. It seemed that the NE was not really changing rapidly but, the science was slightly moving towards better safety, as well as lowering the cost of a nuclear reactor or tower; the cost of these had reached the point of being more than the use of conventional fuels. Then, the difficult choice arose; to undertake a facility taking 6-8 years, with unknown inflation in the meantime, to 'blow out' any contract costs, either making the venture incomplete or scaled down to an unacceptable size, considering the assets at risk.

Dave wanted to learn as much about these problems as possible; hoping to escalate himself up professionally to either, Nuclear Contract Engineer by more schooling, or by experience. Georgia Power was developing a new facility in Burke Co, Georgia with 6 Towers based on a 9year construction period; it was possible that he would be able to study under the present Nuclear Engineers, as this energy mechanism was not declining. He must, however, move quickly, by gaining a base of knowledge sufficient to recommend him to the present nuclear supervisors.

This is to say that they did not have time together to converse and plan for their futures. They played a game called 'Who Am I?', in which one determined that they would be a creature from history, from 1776 till the present, in 10year increments, listing their occupation or place in history along with the category or field in which their fame was earned. The other of them could ask any question but was limited to 4. A few figures were selected by one from the Revolution, several from 1893 to 1842; a greater number from 1843 to 1865. It was a continuing game, a ton of fun, with the night's winner requesting any favor from the loser. There were limits on the favors.

Morgan went through the Spring easily, with a cooperating class of Seniors assisting her in finishing their high school days on a positive note. One asks her "Miss Mitchell, are you and Mr. Dave chaperoning at the Junior-Senior?" M "I don't know; we haven't been requested but are normally available". Student "you both are requested now" Morgan "we accept; please hold the number of flasks down". The students laughed. Morgan addressed them "You know what a wonderful year this has been for all of us; your help has made my job a lot easier and I know that all of you can and will be successful in your future endeavors".

Morgan said to Dave "We're asked to chaperone the Junior-Senior dance and I said aye; OK with you?" Dave "You know that it is". Everyone knew that there had always been a bit of drinking at this event, but usually it was minimum and no one became unruly. This year should be no different if they kept an eye on a few of the boys. Dave "I'll be especially vigilant for over indulgence or erratic behavior". Morgan "thank you; I can advise you whom to watch.

The quarter slipped down to two events; the Junior- Senior and graduation day. The former went well with only one Senior falling prey to Mr. Barleycorn; he was sobered up in the gym showers in order that he not wreck his Dad's car or get in trouble for imbibing. Morgan "good job, Dave, may I count on you next year?". Dave "my darling, I am at your call; whether as a 'bouncer' or as a valet". Moving on to the Graduation; it was relatively sedate until the students started receiving their diplomas WHEN the supporters of each began the racket, loud shouts, clapping, perhaps a fire alarm or some additional device. Morgan "I'm glad that these minutes are over and these kids can enjoy their new status; the audience was no better or worse; this might be their price of admission".

Another Summer was in SW Georgia; a season of growing, harvesting and marketing; busy times for nearly all in Prosperity. Morgan had not lined up anything but the CC in Sylvester and felt that this might be better for her, after years of piling on the work. Dave agreed "darling, you might want to ease up this Summer; you can spend more time with your parents and we might go to Europe or the Mediterranean". Morgan "overseas this year? I hadn't thought about it but it sounds good; let's look at some travel brochures and think it over". Dave "great".

Morgan enjoyed getting out of the attire of a teacher and wearing shorts, halter, a cap and a pair of great Adidas, size 8, for her footsies. Dave "whistling at her outfit, asking, what is the penalty for stalking a barely clad maiden?" Morgan "I would say a filet at the Elks Club in Tifton; including tip and wine, $30.00. not a penny less". Dave "what a sentence to hand down to a lecherous young man". Morgan "take him away to the dungeon; he is a career offender". Both laughed and hugged each other.

Morgan and her Mother were able to be together quite often this Summer, doing the Mother-Daughter things that had been missing for several years; it was a nice change for her; she enjoyed it and told her Mother that. Morgan "Mom, I know how lonesome it is for you and Dad when my time is taken up; and I plan to include you two from now on. Since Marsha can't come down often from Augusta to visit; we just have to arrange our lives to include all of us". Mom "Morgan, no one has worked harder these years than you to build a career, help students and improve our educational system; your Dad and I understand about this; your career comes first and you have not neglected us".

Now and then, Morgan and Mom went to Tifton or Cordele just to have lunch and shop or look in the ladies' boutiques. Styles were changing and not for the better for some ladies; the miniskirts were in vogue and for ladies with large knees or thighs, these lengths were devastating. Morgan declared "Mom, those miniskirts make me feel like I don't have all my clothes on". Mom "You don't". Still, some females insisted on donning a half-frock not designed for their bodies; some of the men recoiled in horror when the misshapen ladies appeared in these 'stylish' creations.

Whatever happened in this gigantic farming area; the heat and humidity remained; stepping outside invited the perspiration to ingulf the body, soaking one's clothes in no time flat. The toilers of the soil were the few who tolerated it to any degree but, they, too, often wished to be in Alaska. The ladies, when dressed for church or a social occasion, repelled this invasion of their bodies/clothing by running from an airconditioned house to an a/c car and, later, to another a/c building. It appeared to affect the facial area and the armpits first, creating very wet spots under the arms, not exactly the delicate image desired.

A stranger asked “where is Prosperity”; an old timer replied” adjacent to Hell”; an accurate comparison. All ‘got by’, some better than others; the early football practices in August were brutal from the humidity, however the early games were as bad. How a player played both offense and defense is beyond belief.

Some way, these Georgians and the tourists wandering off the interstates, survived another Summer of rainstorms, that increased the humidity, the soiling of clothing by perspiration and the discomfort of 100degree heat. Thank you, Lord, for the Fall.

At times, if it was not stifling, they had social events outside, but the wise ones stuck to inside facilities with a/c. The only advantage to an outside meeting was the briefness. One Summer in this geographical area for outsiders was enough to steer them to the mountains and the beaches.

Morgan and Dave were local so they rarely complained about the weather unless it failed to rain; bad for the crops, the driver of the local economy. Morgan stayed with her abbreviated outfits, to the enjoyment of all men, who were privileged to observe her. She wore any garment with grace and charm, a creature of style and charm although she seemed unaware of her attributes. Others were not.

Occasionally, around the end of August, on one of the large farms, they would have a peanut boiling, just as its stated; new peanuts were washed, put in a boiler with salt and cooked until they were softer. Almost everyone liked this little ground product and ate them until their belts had to be loosened. After cooking, there were sold on the public streets, in stores and vegetable stands. People outside the South ate theirs ‘parched’ or roasted; not bad but the boiled ones whetted the appetites of the residents.

Somehow, they got through this scorching heat with their sanity, by the end of September, acting normal at times. Most evenings, Morgan and Dave were together but did frequent Lake Blackshear, near Cordele. Their friends had a speed boat, suitable for water skiing; being pulled at the end of a long rope by the boat, while standing (hopefully) on the polished wooden skis. It looked good but there could be issues with the lake, the rope or the skier. Dave was a decent athlete and had skied before, BUT this was another day. e lake was down due to the paucity of rain, normally not a problem as long as the skier stayed in the main channel. At times the direction of the boat, could limit an average participant's ability to avoid the shallower areas; this happened to Dave. He was going well as the boat reached a curve in the channel, throwing Dave very close o the shore where a piece of a downed tree was just below the water line. OOPS, Dave went head over cup, the skis floating free as the boat continued; the occupants oblivious to the accident. They retrieved Dave from the water but one leg was strained, sidelined for three weeks. The Medicos say that a break is easier to treat than a sprain, strain or muscle pull. He did receive a 'boot' shortly to enable his mobility. This was his right leg so the driving was up to Morgan; or she was 'up' to the driving. His wonderful couple had avoided any mishaps so far but the odds caught up to them.

Back at school, Morgan chafed under the clothing deemed 'appropriate' for an educator; her time this summer had 'spoiled' her with its casualness and freedom. But, the machine of education now had control; those dresses would be worn as uniforms are. Morgan knew the drill so she kept it inside, only discussing the matter with close friends with small mouths and silent tongues. She still had the Seniors; maybe the best class but still capable of creating a few headaches; lost textbooks, missing raincoat, a couple of Mothers who desired to direct their child's educational matters. Not serious but disrupting.

Morgan was now teaching the siblings of her earlier students; who were likely to be the opposites of their older brothers/sisters. Not a problem, just an observation by Morgan. The holidays of Christmas

2003 were approaching; at the community college at her last session of the year; the students presented her with a .22 revolver, after obtaining special permission to gift it. Morgan was overwhelmed with their generosity BUT did accept it.

Morgan hung on to her community college position; the middle-aged students solidly in her corner; not receptive to other instructors. She enjoyed the mature conversations held with her pupils; the give and take as well as their varied experiences with suspects who became criminals. They knew that you can't always tell a book by its cover; the mildest one might possess a stock of poison to settle a score with his wife or someone else. The type of murderer, rapist or assaulter was often not 'according to a normal profile'. This created more difficulties for the investigator, how does one select from the entire population? Of course, DNA has simplified some investigative issues but not all; therefore the 'serial' criminal continues his spree until his MO (modus operandi, method of operation) is validated. Morgan learned as she taught these experts; there is no sure and quick route to solving a serious crime.

Morgan's discussion with her Psychology pupils at the WCC took this line: Morgan "Lt. Jones, you have a homicide occurring in the back yard of the residence; the deceased was shot with a .22 pistol in the head. No DNA, no prints, no witnesses; deceased had no criminal record; what do you do?" Jones "you must develop a character for the deceased, by interviewing neighbors, a wife, fellow employees at his job location and his Pastor, if any. Habits, haunts, associates other than listed and female companions". Morgan "well done, the basic research on an unknown, looking for perhaps a motive first, then a suspect; the logical way to approach or initiate an investigation of this type case".

Morgan felt that 'she had become an amateur sleuth these past few years but knew that she, personally, had only scratched the surface. She mused "CIs are made, not born". Very true. Morgan had enrolled in a self- defense course in Prosperity; the teaching was first, how to avoid confrontation; secondly, how to escape if accosted and finally, how to fight, if cornered. She felt reasonably confident with her skills but knew that if the aggressor was overly strong or had an accomplice; she could be overmatched. The one trick that they taught in the case of an aggressor attacking one leaving their car was 'to throw the keys or any object' at the intruder AND run.

The policemen gave her sound advice on self-protection and survival, as she wondered about the necessity of learning all this; Prosperity was as secure as Fort Knox. Her psyche drove Morgan to intake any matter that had any slight chance of being relevant to her welfare.

At Christmas, her WCC students gave her a.22 automatic, after obtaining permission from the school; she accepted with grace, acknowledging their generosity. She put it in the glove compartment of her car, temporarily putting it out of her mind. She did not encourage any giving of her Seniors; they'd need all their resources later in the Spring, I.e. prom and graduation, not including 'the Spring Break'.

She and Dave were practical for once; she gave him a miniature nuclear tower with removable parts; he gave her .22 ammo and a large orange scarf like the aviators wore. Mom and Dad got their usual thoughtful gifts of 'necessary' items; they acted as if Morgan had given them gifts of myrrh and incense. Anyway, the season passed us into 2004, the 4th year after 9-11, the worst tragedy in American civilian history. Morgan "it will never end in the Middle East and Bud might have to go again, God forbid".

Bud did not contact her; she thought of it, putting the matter at Bud's occupation with his business. Or was it Bud's respect for Dave? Either reason was acceptable to Morgan. She still considered him a friend but the passionate times were in the rearview mirror. There was no thought in her of ever being more than friends; once the matter was concluded, it WAS over. The marriage needed to be resurrected and discussed; if Dave went to Burke County, adjacent to Augusta, Georgia, it would take some thought before she departed her home to set up a new residence. Morgan, worrying "would this looming event upset her future?"

Morgan did not long remain less than optimistic; after all, the important events in her life had always worked out to her benefit. She then thought "but don't we lose control of our lives at some point, after maturity?" Good thought, the answer is MAYBE. As Morgan was so busy during the week, her deep reflecting generally took place on the weekends. Not so deflating but enough to awake one to the uncertainty of life.

All her students returned to the school; not always did this occur as many families locally, moved with their jobs or farmers, who had given up on the land. This class was eager, responsible, and resourceful; likely to set a few records at old PHS. No changes in Morgan's approach to teaching these 'almost' adults; just stick to the meat and potatoes of education, let the 'movers' do their things, while the experienced teachers did the work.

CHAPTER XII: LIFE HAPPENS

It was hard to believe that 2003 was closing; she had been teaching six years but it felt like much more; Morgan was still focused on her career, a marriage and a family; all were working for her. The Fall was beautiful as usual, the leaves colored most of those of crayons; the old hardwoods in the forests came out with new brightness, giving hope to all who resided in this great land. The farmers or planters (the larger acreage) had a very good season with bumper crops; so big that a few pessimists wondered if all their abundance could be marketed? No problem; the foreign markets were open to America's products, the lowest to produce in the world. As the returns poured back to the producers, they were just conduits for the returns directed to farm equipment manufacturers, improved seeds/plants, fertilizers and insecticides. Costs were up but the sales kept pace with inflation. If farming seemed easy, that was a mirage; this was still risky business.

As the tillers of the earth received, so did they reinvest most of their net into the local economy; clothing, autos, kitchen machines and entertainment electronics were high on the list. Entering the holiday season, it was apparent that this area would celebrate in style, compensating for a couple of less than robust profits. Dave and Morgan decided to forego exchanging gifts; electing to contribute to one or two families recommended by the Families and Childrens Service. Of course, it would be anonymous, with the parents being the donors, the only real way to maintain Christmas traditions.

Morgan and Dave went shopping in Prosperity this year as a few new stores were opened, providing a larger selection for local purchasing. Morgan "Dave, what do I buy for Mom and Dad? I'm about out of ideas; help me out, please". Dave "How about a secretary for your Mom's bedroom and a computer for your Dad to work with?" M "Dave, your mind works like a machine; I put in ideas and you put out solutions". That solved the problems for Morgan.

Now, there was time for really enjoying the Christmas break; no frantic last-minute buying or acid stomach over the gifts' receptions. Morgan and Dave kidded each other, acting like teenagers, and enjoying each minute of the playfulness. He was still working on a position in Burke County but not quite ready to spring his resume' on the Vogtle leadership. Morgan loved her life with its rewards, pleasantness, friends and bright future. She still kept her diary, each day; if diverted one day, she caught up the next; her notes were more positive almost every year. Only the major breakup with Bud had interfered with her tranquility, but it was necessary and she had not looked back.

Time flies when romance or cheerfulness is in the air; the season was closing on January 2d, 2004. Dave and Morgan decided to go to a New Year's Eve bash in Tifton at the Elk Lodge; a rarity for the two but hard work does have its rewards. A great band at the Lodge; they were paired with a young couple from Tifton; the interchange was very pleasant. All four played "Do you know so and so?" In such a small area of our two towns; there was a match of many people known by at least two of us. The band played until 1 minute after mid night; all sang

Auld Lang Syne. Although we had a filet for dinner, a trip to the Waffle House was in order. The four of us, dressed to the hilt, strolled into the WH, selected a booth and proceeded to obtain waffles; never better. Afterwards, we bid them good night and headed for Worth County.

January 2d was a work day; Dave dropped her off at her house, then scooted to his. The next morning was informed that the local NG Engineer Company was re-deploying to the Middle East; that meant Bud also. After school her phone rang; it was Bud, telling Morgan what she already knew, that he was departing on Jan 4th with the unit;" he would be in Prosperity a day early to say goodbye to his Mom and Dad; could she come over to his house to perhaps ease the strain?" Morgan "Sure, Bud, I'll be glad to, what time?" Bud "maybe1:30, just for a few minutes".

Out of school at 1P, Morgan drove to Bud's house; his car was there; it had been a long time since she'd seen him so this could be touchy. She walked up to the front door, hit the bell and Bud appeared "Hi, Morgan, please come on in". Morgan to Bud "you look good, Bud; it's been awhile". Bud "these last two years have really been something: life throws a screwball now and then". M "Bud, you know it; one gets set, they think, for a career; then things change quickly, frequently not for the better". M "Bud, what do you want me to say to your parents?" Bud "something like 'we need soldiers like Bud to fight for this country; I know that it's dangerous but important sacrifices are not free; he's smart and will come through with our prayers". Morgan "That was great, Bud, it's what I feel, just comforting your parents is worth it all".

His parents walked in, quiet, thoughtful and, of course, sad. Morgan "I'm here to support you in this sendoff of Bud; without men like him, this country could be much worse off". His Dad "Morgan, you know how much we think of you; your common sense is worth a ton to his Mother and myself; you can pray regularly for him, if you will?" M "you know that I will, often and earnestly; you need to be with him now so I'll run on; you know how to reach me; take care Bud". Morgan "I'll be with you Bud, even if you walk through the Valley of Death; be careful; I'll write to you". She left before she started crying, something that she seldom permitted herself to do.

Morgan was glad that the meeting was over and she had done everything in her power to comfort his parents. She would pray for his safety often. It was nice that her teaching kept her so busy that this matter and others were moved to the back of her brain. She just jumped into both positions; welcoming the law enforcement officers and her Seniors. Of course, Dave had his time with her but there was little for others in her life. Every day was similar to the last; the hours flew by as Morgan used all her knowledge to insure, that ALL her pupils learned as much as possible in the time available. She had little opportunity to clutter her mind up with painful issues, thank goodness. She had never been more proficient in her duties and both classes recognized her expertise. Yes, Morgan was achieving all of her dreams of having a great education and using it to benefit others.

This quarter was going as the sands in the hourglass; constantly, regularly and despite any other events. Morgan was bearing down on the Psychology dealing with aberrant behavior and its relationship to criminal acts. Her older students really enjoyed this area of her course; primarily as it would be of great benefit to them in their chosen work. Her use of examples from actual crimes added the realism that made the course so valuable. This class asked more questions than any high school group; trying to squeeze as much information out as the course permitted.

These little exercises kept the class alert as they wanted to learn the methodology for solving crimes; not maintaining their current procedures of solving crimes by the 'dragnet' system of spreading a wide net, wasting time by interviewing witnesses not even slightly connected to the case. It was apparent that many officers were just put into investigations from the uniform divisions, without the intense instruction in; how to properly undertake an investigation. Yes, on TV, it appeared to be so simple BUT was not, in most cases. Time was the ingredient that needed to be properly conserved AND these classes were intended to accomplish precisely that,

For Morgan, the classes at the high school were, for the most part, tattooed on her brain; she could teach them without extra education or effort. History did revolve but the texts were some years behind the reported events. This was not an obstacle as the subject as printed, covered, at the least, one to two centuries.

Finishing up Winter quarter, Morgan felt pleased with the class progress, knowing that Spring might bring a small delay to the progress. The 'break' arrived and the students flew out of the building to rev up their jalopies, and get the smoke in the air as they disappeared for 7 days. Morgan and Dave had thought about the break and decided to just stay around Prosperity this year. Unless they went to Europe, Morgan did not want to travel in such a short time, having to rush back to school. What would they do? She thought, "we could just get a cabin at Lake Blackshear; swim, fish, dine out and just be with one another without a crowd".

Dave did say that he needed to go to Waynesboro, Burke County, to submit his application, "would she go?" Morgan, without knowing the area, stated "Dave, I think that I'll stay here; what could I do around a nuclear plant?" Dave "good question; it is isolated from civilization, and you might be bored; I know what that means". Morgan laughed "Dave, you are getting better in analyzing my thoughts; anyway, my cell works fine". Case settled.

Morgan spent a day or two going through her clothing, separating out the fashioned garments and others not worn since the 'cold war'; giving them to the 'clothes closet' at the church. She needed more space to BUY more garments, Go figure.

Morgan avoided the news of the Iraq-Afghan fighting; she dreaded any notice of her friend being injured or even worse. "damn it, there were others who had never seen a uniform and they were where? Under the bed or hiding in their family's barn? This was a hell of a mess; these desert engagements with fools who sought death". She, moving on, denied the devil or whoever, the satisfaction of watching her grieve prematurely. Morgan had the ability to switch emotional gears easily, abandoning any negative thoughts; focusing on her present and future,

At Lake Blackshear, the two did as planned; fished, swam, read, relaxed and nightly, at the lake 'fish house', ate either fish dishes, pizza or barbecue. This intake of calories caused a shift in their diets at breakfast and lunch, to a sandwich and unsweetened tea. These diets were not punishing nor starving; just a bit less than usual. She and Dave had not been by themselves in some time AND this was pleasant, to enjoy each other uninhibited and free.

The Lake was only a couple of miles from Cordele, so they rode in one afternoon to a steak house; later enjoying a filet on the patio, under the oaks. This was great living, down South, if not under the Magnolias, then the oaks and sycamores. It was hot already around Southwest Georgia, AND shortly, would be as a furnace. Riding with the A/C on was good as we scanned the watermelon fields of this farming county, Crisp, formed around 1915 from portions of Worth and Dooly counties.

Everything ends, so does the 'break', and Dave and Morgan leave their sanctuary, the lake among the pines. Now, more education for her Seniors and Law Enforcement guys. Actually, at this time Morgan was so entranced by her 'jobs' that she missed those groups when she was away. Not unusual for many who actually love their work; and their pupils REALLY love them. The kids were on Cloud 9 or at least 8, as their 1st day of Spring began; jawing with their mates about the events of these past few days, MAYBE telling or implying a number of escalated instances with girls. Not unusual, but expected of young roosters.

Morgan gave a full quarter of very good history to all who came near, prompting their better responses to her succinct questioning. With all the winnowing out of History from curriculums during this period of 'burn the books', it was pleasing to most to view Morgan's tutoring of this fine graduating class. Morgan was so enthralled with her success that she put on the final test, the question "what may we do to bring back to public institutions, history as we once knew it?" IT was a 20point question.

It appeared that she and Dave, as usual, would chaperone the Junior-Senior Prom; hopefully, this would find most boys (and girls) with empty flasks, at the beginning rather than at the end. The other concern for Morgan were the fast automobiles that the young men treasured AND might race on the country roads, with their hills and curves. Morgan said "Girl, quit borrowing trouble".

The termination of the year was arriving rapidly, only awaiting the Baccalaureate on Sunday night and the Graduation on Monday night. No surprises for Morgan on her grading; ALL made it; no holdovers. It was as hot as blazes during these last few days. Morgan dreaded the post-planning at school; it might be well done, but at what inconvenience? She didn't dwell long on this subject, thinking about the possibility for the Summer.

With the usual hot weather, Morgan, after her final week of school, went to shorts and a Tee for the duration, working around her house; a bit of painting, another furniture item and additional insulation for the attic. Of course, she and Dave ate together at least 4 nights a week; she exercised two afternoons at the local fitness center; she had started going to church again; Dave was a bit slow on this.

The story is told about the boy who left Worth Co. at a young age, telling all "don't change anything in this county until I return". He did return in 25 years, offering "well, you didn't". This could be said about many or most of the 45 counties; in fact, a number of counties had their economy in reverse; the young leaving, houses vacant, businesses gone; a village subsisting on social security and retirement checks; even churches cutting their services or closing. No thought of county mergers for reasons outlined before.

Morgan went to the 'young' adults' functions by herself when Dave was at Vogtle or out of town for Georgia Power. It was not uncomfortable for her at all; a number there were single. She enjoyed herself very much except for the humidity; how does one outrun that? It is said by some elderly citizens that 'sweating' is good for one, but as Morgan thought of the ruined dresses, especially under the arms and on the backs, that she had endured before proms and beauty contests; she had to disagree. Worse was to want to hold her date's hand or cup his cheek, but could not as her palms were dripping salt water. No sir, this whole 45 county area needed to be air conditioned, with the ability of the female to lower the temperature at any time.

But, it did seem that AC was on the way, at least in the stores and houses; the autos had it for some time. Morgan's house had central AC where one could be comfortable at all times.

CHAPTER XIII: FLOWS AS THE RIVER

The summer of 2004 came to an end; Morgan was ready for life and all its uncertainties; at least she was in her 'den', protected and experienced in life. As she analyzed herself, she saw two Morgans; the adolescent one arriving from Ashburn 14years ago compared to the 29year old, mature beauty; experienced in education, psychology and personal relations. Her mental gymnastics reminded her of Margaret Mitchell's, GONE WITH THE WIND, a movie in 1937, the world's premiere in Atlanta in 1938 when: one said to Scarlett O'Hara (Vivien Leigh, British) something about her soft and kind nature as a younger lady. She responded" That girl doesn't exist anymore" referring to her experiences in and after the War, her two marriages to men that she did not love, as well as her avaricious nature.

In days past, when movie stars were admired, babies were named after them and many lived and breathed the lives of each. Morgan, logically, had dreamed or focused her mind, at times, on her future in or around the movies or television productions. Where had she misstepped? She had intimate (a codeword) and deep relationships with two fine men; most women were very fortunate to even have one. The second guessing of herself and her history, went on, with no logical answers. Marsha, her sister, was settled in Augusta, with 'silent' Wayne, her husband, specialist in internal medicine but not communication. Morgan couldn't dump this on her; this was self-inflicted, homemade, not manufactured. Morgan 'soldiered' on with her pack full of 'what ifs', 'maybes' and her faults.

September was there and she was back in her familiar spot; riding herd on the Seniors. In football, she compared to the Safety Man, properly said, as he/she had the final shot at those trying to cross the goal, whether getting 6 points or a diploma. In honesty, there was no gain in the last class in high school holding back a couple who were likely to offer difficulty to whomever taught them later. Morgan did take pride in her 100% graduation record, only missing a couple of times, by reason of sickness or accidents. Whether all the graduates were active and productive citizens or NOT; they did not frequent Prosperity HS, except for football contests.

Since the age gap between Morgan and her pupils had widened, she felt that the boys had given up on her being their pinup or Junior-Senior date. Not so, in earlier years; most were cautious enough to avoid direct statements in her hearing, about her 'sexy' look, boyfriends, etc. However, their looks sent a message of raw lust, not punishable but recordable in the memory.

This class of 2005 was mostly interested in finishing the year as easily as possible; Morgan, in time, had outrun the juvenile desires of the most aggressive male pupils, thank goodness. Boys can be boys but not men until the maturity overcomes them. The Fall quarter was uneventful; the usual faculty duties at the football games took some of Morgan's time and, the school bus checkout ate up the rest during the days. Dave could come back from Waynesboro as his varied schedule permitted; however, it was so erratic, that she was unable to count on much of his time if she did go here. While she was not a wanderer, in the social sense, she did not like to be constantly alone; only the engagement ring protected her from a multitude of propositions, phone calls and likely crude words. What does she do? Life, for her and most, is a series of forks in the road; if enough of these are presented, the individual is likely to eventually take the wrong fork.

It is a given now in society that living alone is not the better way to make one's way through life; however, she could not take in another lady as her privacy is too valuable. As for a man; even if she wanted to have someone, her job would not permit it; the next 15 years reversed that policy. Morgan was very logical but the situations facing her, and most, are often illogical; the average bloke in Georgia would surmise that she was the most contented lady around; beautiful, composed, bright, congenial; her superlatives could go on. Her thought processes were not flawed, but she, as most, was thinking of tomorrow, not today; an unsettling exercise for any, especially one who had accomplished so much in a brief period.

Morgan always put on her best face to all other than her parents; as they have viewed their children in sickness and in health; in plenty and in less; so they had been there, seeing the real Morgan. A dreamer, as her, always suffers more disappointment than a plodder; imagining the best is to many, almost like having it. But not in reality. Most, when faced with complexities, seek another, likely of the same sex, to 'unload upon', but in a small town, that's often difficult.

Regardless of problems, the sands of time, sift through and the quarter was ending, holiday break to vary the same routine. Her community college schedule did not end until 4 days or so after the HS let out. This class was greatly different from some of the others; younger detectives, a couple of handsome guys. One, in particular, caught Morgan's eye; a neat man, quiet, thoughtful and eager to learn. He was always interested in the subject matter. Before the WCC shut down for the holidays, he came to her at the recess; introduced himself, Gene Phillips from Tifton; Morgan "I know who you are; remember, I take the roll". Gene blushed, as he always conducted himself with dignity, G "I love the course but have a bit of difficulty with Chapter 4, "The other persona inside", you know; multiple bodies in one body". Morgan laughed "you mean the number of personalities contained by a few patients?" Gene "Yes, you have it". Morgan "the class will be over soon; we can sit here and discuss it; do you have a suggestion?" G "Maybe have a cup of coffee at the Waffle House?". Morgan "sounds fine".

After class they went to the local WH, sat in a booth, with their coffee and talked briefly about themselves; primarily Gene. Then they discussed the issues outlined earlier, clarifying them for Gene. They were there about 35 minutes; then both went to their cars, after a goodnight. Morgan, on her way home, thought, "this was unusual, my actually being out with a pupil; then her logic kicked in; it wasn't a date; it was a tutoring session, that's all".

CHAPTER XIV: LIFE SOURS

The quarter began as usual, slowly after the lazy days of Christmas; but her experience level was much higher; therefore, the class should advance rapidly. One small issue; the Class only wanted to graduate in June 2005 not set any academic records. With this quality of material, Morgan could almost guarantee that her class might set an academic record..

Morgan sailed through the quarter with no work-related issues but Bud Stanborough, her former student, approached the ticket booth, where she was working at the football game.

He was not profane but his attitude was not that of pupil t teacher; it was teasing in a crude way. He started with "Miss Morgan, remember me; your favorite student?" M "Bud, I remember you from the Senior class; what are you doing now?" Bud, "working with my uncle on his farm; he has pecan orchards also; he's a smooth operator". M "I'll bet; and you are learning a lot?" B "I already knew most of it". M "do you have a girlfriend now?" Bud "No, I'm waiting for you". Morgan "You're too old for me and I'm engaged". B "Age is not the main thing and the engagement is just an agreement to agree". Morgan "Bud, I have to work now, goodbye".

After he departed Morgan thought" he's bigger now and has that full beard; wonder whom his riding partner is and where they hang out?". She was not alarmed but it seemed strange to her that he still picked her out of the crowd; she had an idea 'what, If I ask one of the Deputies to just check on his record?" And maybe she was just on edge since Dave was not here. It left her mind

At the Worth Community College, she did talk to one of the Worth deputies, who agreed to run a check on him and ask the Chief of Police if Bud had any trouble around town. Then Morgan put it in the back recesses of her brain. School zipped along; basketball was in season and many liked that better than football. She talked to Dave at least every other day BUT it was not like being together. The old saying was: absence makes the heart grow fonder (for someone else).

Morgan tired of being alone; almost like being a widow; she heard that her Bud would be home by mid-Summer along with the Engineer Company; good news, if he can dodge those homemade IEDs, then return in one piece, her prayers would be answered. Now and then she stopped by his house to try to cheer up his parents. The whole town was involved as the 125 men all came from Worth county; Morgan heard that a unit or two from the surrounding areas, had suffered heavily in an ambush. It's clear that a small town can suffer greatly if only a few are KIA or WIA.

Some of the troopers enrolled at the college asked about Bud, as they had played football with him or knew him in high school; he was still high on their totem pole as they remembered his great leadership. Morgan thought with bitter sweet memories "what I'd give to do that period over".

Morgan spent so much time alone at her home, that her mind delved into the past 10 years constantly, bringing to the surface many events. It was upsetting for the negative ones to emerge before those of a positive nature. She told herself to “snap out of it’.

When Morgan and Dave talked, it sometimes didn’t end well; maybe she wasn’t alert to his issues AND he was unaware of hers. Sounds easy but is relatively hard. She hoped he’d be home soon BUT when. She was teaching at the WCC one evening about dark and, again at the break, Gene said “Miss Mitchell, can you help me again with an issue or two on criminal insanity?” Morgan “I think so, Gene: will it take long?” Gene “I don’t think so but the line between understanding the proceedings and legal insanity, has me wrapped”.

At the break, Morgan “do you want to talk here after class is over?” Gene “I’ve been cooped up all day with paperwork; is it ok if we do as last time and go to the Waffle House?” Morgan was ok with that; she needed to relax also. They were in the WH in a booth, as usual, sipping their coffees; jus to be polite, Morgan asked him about his job (deputy) and just a little about his personal life.

He replied about both; only slighting his personal situation. Morgan did not pry or ask any further. They worked out a good statement of the issue that he had asked about. Before they left, Gene asked her if she was engaged. Morgan nodded. G “where is your fiancee’?”An innocent enough question. M “he’s an engineer employed at the nuclear plant near Augusta”. He nodded seriously and Morgan dismissed it.

They went outside and he just said “Morgan, you help me so much; may I do something for you sometime?” Morgan thought: this is innocent enough o I’ll agree “Gene, that would be fine”. He saw her to the car; said ‘goodnight” and departed. Morgan, driving home, mused about, Mr. Gene “was he real? Was it all about her OR the coffee?” She was good about categorizing people but was he Brand X, a generic substitute for an original?” It wouldn’t be long, if he wanted her, before he made his play; she certainly knew that approach. Inside, she pondered the motive’ or reason, as the Detectives did, attempting to try her knowledge in this dilemma. In other times, the motive was the first thing sought, after the cause of death, in a homicide case. Other crimes were usually more evident as to causation. Drugs illegal, had caused the search for motives to take a back seat; many drug crimes were nutty, beyond normal comprehension. She rolled over, sleeping as the exhausted.

School, both categories, were progressing, as Morgan used, more and more recorded cases at the WCC and played 'what if' with the History class. What if this country did this instead of the alternative? Would this country be as large and strong? Many variations of this theme; the classes rose to the bait, eager to solve her, at times, difficult question. Dave called the next day; he wanted to come over for a day and night, if he could; was it OK? Morgan agreed; it was past time for them to determine if they would take the next step and, if so, when? She was tired of the loneliness, the constant delays, not all his fault, and not being married, with at least one child; like other girls her age. NOW that she said it, she felt much better. It was likely to be a spirited conversation between these two.

Dave was arriving late that afternoon so she left the house unlocked when she left for night school, so that Dave could get in. She finished at WCC about 8PM, arriving around 8:40 at home. Dave's car was parked beside the driveway; inside he was reading the newspaper, sitting in a sitting room rocker. As he heard her car motor, he rose, washed his hands and greeted her at the door, kissing her on the cheek. They started making small talk, laughing, perhaps to avoid anxiety. It wasn't long before the talk became more serious; "we're here" said Dave and "we want to be here; what do you think?" Morgan, used to the engineer spiel, responded" You're basically right but neither Prosperity or Waynesboro is going to move without impetus. Who supplies that?" Dave "both of us do by visiting back and forth till your schools finish in June; then you come for the summer". M "sounds simple, Dave; it looks good but feels bad; I can't just lay down my responsibilities and career to traipse to an alien area, completely unknown, to me; can you not see that?" Dave "I realize that this might be a sacrifice to both of us but what else might we do?" Morgan took off her engagement ring for the first time, other than bathing, "Dave we need a time out; it's not fair to either of us the way it's going; a breather is warranted. I can't wear the ring under the current conditions; and you are tied also; listen to me, please?" Dave appeared shocked but, in reality, was likely relieved that they were severing, at least for the time being. He "Morgan, perhaps you're right; to permit this to fester into a real controversy would not beneficial for either of us. Let's try a 6month separation; either can call the other or not. Either may go out or not; if something is getting serious, then a call will be made to the other". Morgan was surprised but not astounded at his words; she felt relief. Dave "it's better that I leave tonight in order to initiate the agreement; I do want this to work but we'll see". Morgan "thanks, Dave, let's try on this. good night". It was not easy for Morgan to go to sleep BUT she knew from her past that once a decision, however difficult, is made, much of the pressure is off. And it was. She had not been so cheery in some time. At school, she radiated as she had a reasonable chance of now living a normal life; her thought was that the 6months delay would morph into a longer period, eventually collapsing. That night, a couple of the men noticed that the ring was missing but did not ask; she did not tell. Morgan thought that the missing ring was a portion of her attire; and she was only partially dressed. After class, one of her friends "Miss Morgan, anything you want to tell us?" She "Soon, Jamie; I just need some time right now". Jamie nodded "we just want you to be happy". Morgan "thanks to you all, I will be, shortly".

Some of the pressure was receding; Morgan seemed as if a new person; her light was shining brightly. Food tasted better, no complaints about life and she was not apprehensive about the future. It was her first time to reflect on the future in months; and so pleasant. Most knew that something had occurred for her betterment; and waited anxiously to know what.

Winter quarter was dwindling rapidly; finals today; then grades posted (by number) on their room door; if U lost your number, too bad. The break was used by some to go to the Florida beaches; others helped on the farms and a few went to Lake Blackshear; the motive of many was NOT to spend money that they could need shortly. Some painted their parents' home, others cleaned their farm equipment and some helped the elderly with their home repairs. Whatever one did, the time flew out of the hourglass till the school bells rang a new.This quarter, Spring, was the favorite of most, Mothers' Day, Easter, the Prom, then graduation weekend. In the meantime, the Seniors were seeking employment for the period June through August. As before, it was a rigorous project as the number of jobs, outside the farms, was not great. Many had to go to Sylvester or Tifton to hope for any help; ignoring Cordele that had the same issues as Prosperity; a few got hired for the first day in June. Were the wages about $7.00 or a tad more? The farms were not controlled by this minimum wage and who, in his right mind, wanted that anyway? It seems that some were acclimated to farming and wanted to continue. So be it.

Employment was good for all; if these youngsters were not working, they would be loafing with all of its temptations and problems. Now and then, the school hired a few to make some repairs on school property, however, some of the local contractors, if they knew, objected to this. It still continued as most cared not how the repairs were done, and cheaply. That was and is he watchword for selecting services or products for use.

Getting through the final 21/2 months of the school year was a snap; most were on their toes, a bit apprehensive about the receipt of a diploma; in fact, the military would now, not accept one without the minimum of a GED. Not exactly a high standard; a barrier 8 inches high that a mouse could jump over. Was Morgan going to be solo at the Jr-Sr Prom? Or would she nab a partner?

Morgan was thinking of Gene but needed to test him again; this time she suggested the tutoring, and he agreed. She planned a light dinner at the VFW for them; it was private and they could talk business or anything else; she asked Gene, whose eyes had fixed on her left hand, likely noticing its barrenness. He agreed as a mutt savors a piece of steak. They departed as the bell rang; leaving a few students to talk among themselves. At the Legion, Morgan noticed a couple of her prior students, lifting a pint at the bar. She waved at each as Gene found a booth; the waitress, in plain clothes, as the detectives allowed, took their orders; she, a hamburger and milk; Gene a BLT and unsweetened tea. The Chef wasn't long; the plates came still in heat, Morgan said grace; Gene bowed his head. Then Morgan began "Gene, how about your wife". Gene, blushing "we're separated for a year now; the future is bleak; I notice that your ring is missing". Morgan "yes, we decided to put it on ice for a while; we can date and mingle. Most seemed to understand".

After that conversation, Morgan was accepted as just one of them, no 'hitting' on her unless she invited it and solely by close friends. She decided to invite Gene to the Prom; she hoped that he had a tuxedo. As she asked him, to go, she let him know that it was formal; with a tux. The night, Gene picked her up in his new Camry, Lexus primary product, at 7:30 P. He was spiffy in his tux with red cummerbund and bow tie. Morgan was a knockout, in one of her prior gowns; they were always in storage to deter the moths, terrible in hot weather. He was the perfect gentleman, opening and closing doors for her; his voice was pleasant, soft and polite; Morgan thought that he was about as good as any guy with his approach to her.

At the Prom, the faculty had a separate area where they gathered; small 4 -person tables. They sat with another young couple, with a good view of the dance floor. Morgan "my gosh I forgot to ask Gene if he danced". As the music began, Gene asked Morgan if she wished to dance. Her reply "I thought that you'd never ask". They laughed. Taking the floor with the youngsters to a ballroom dance, slow but romantic. Gene's touch was light but leading; his grasp of her was polite but steady; he didn't try to drive her breasts into his chest; he was smooth and quick n his feet. Morgan was attentive and admiring; to have a new man NOT mash her twins was refreshing and encouraging. They sat out a dance or two, talking as old friends.

The night flew by as the two danced with the best; both limber and agile. Some of the faculty complimented the two on their performance; Morgan told Gene how well he danced; he seemed embarrassed. No incidents except for two who imbibed in John Barleycorn too heavily; a driver was found for each, to shuttle them home. Just learners and hopefully, paying attention to the problem. Gene and Morgan closed up the gym, the Prom location. Then Gene said softly "the Elks Club is still open; may we go there for a while?" Morgan "I'm having so much fun that I hate to go home". Gene "thank you; this way we can unwind from the dance". Arriving, Gene bought a bottle of light Chilean wine, cooled, and they had a glass or two. The band had closed up but the jukebox was turning out the 'goodies' from the '60s, Elvis, the Fat Man, Jerry Lee Lewis, Patsy Cline; all the hits that boys and girls could agree on. They took a spin or two then just talked to one another. Gene was a superb conversationalist and Morgan held her own.There were very few at that time in the Elks Club; the evening was great. Then the employee cut off the jukebox; it was time to close. On the way to Morgan's, they were both quiet, just going over the entire evening.; her house was in front of them. Gene turned off the car, opened her door for her, easing her out. They were only steps from her door; Morgan asked "would you like to come in, Gene?". Him "Morgan, it's late and you have neighbors, can we do that later?" Morgan, surprised but pleased, said "I'll hold you to it, Gene". As he turned, he held her, kissing her lightly on the lips; she returned the kiss, so pleasant and welcome. He returned to his car, saluting her as he went; in a second, he was gone. Inside, Morgan set for a while, just thinking of his manners; his Mother or someone had certainly worked diligently to inculcate in him these values. She thought that he was one of a thousand.

Her weekend was unplanned but the 'youngsters' had something planned at one of the barns all over the county. Ringing Gene, he was up, having coffee; spoke in his soft voice" didn't I just see you a couple of hours ago?" Morgan "she might have been my sister or my Mother". Gene "hardly". He picked her up at 7:30 for the country outing with square dancing; all talked about this folk dance but few knew the moves. The first thing at the barn was to take just a few instructions; easy enough, as the instructor was a talented operator of a dance academy. After this, the band started easily, Morgan and Gene catching on right away. Three sets or so was adequate for both, as they sipped cider and ate apple cake. Morgan introduced Gene around and, suddenly, he was a part of this group. Their events were usually by 10, leaving a bit of time for something else.

As they departed the farm, Gene "My dear, what would you like to do?" Morgan was surprised as rarely did a date seek her advice BUT Gene was not the average date. Morgan "let's go to my house and listen to the stereo?" G "well said, my Dear; my steed is headed that way". They pulled into her drive, parked and exited, Morgan unlocked her door, both going inside. The stereo was in the sitting room, along with a couch, on which they sat. The stereo played softly classical music as 'Greensleeves', Mozart, Wagner, and the Boston String Orchestra, all superb contributors.

Sitting and listening, Morgan sat close to him so that his arm and hand, had to be around her. She leaned over, kissing him with a full kiss, her red lipstick, tattooing his lips. He was not bashful now, returning her energy fully, a complete kiss. There were more; his mouth had a pleasant taste, gentle but firm; the object of a girl's desire. He went no further and neither knew precisely what the other was thinking, the best possible. At times with unknown person, words may come slowly, but not this time. Morgan kept it going as they discussed many topics except themselves. Gene gave some of his background, a native of another county nearer to Florida; a law enforcement officer for ten years; with 2 years of college. Married for three years, only lived together two of those years. No children, no dependents, lived alone. He knew about Morgan; she was a household name in this area; from her younger days.

Around one am. Gene stood up, "Morgan this is great BUT you need your sleep so I'll call you in the later A.M." Morgan "Gene, you're right, let's call it a night".

And they did, Gene departing and Morgan prepared herself for bed, now sleepy and ready for the sandman to come. And he did.

It was Sunday, Morgan had not been regular in attending church; she thought that if she went with another, she could regain her regularity for church. Calling Gene, he responded "Morgan, I'll be there in 20; be ready. She was and they slipped in at 1100 on the dot; having to go down near the front to find seats. It was always thought that this practice was to punish the late comers, but for ladies attired to the 'hilts', it was an Easter walk. Letting them observe her in her best and her escort, nattily attired himself, was the ultimate reward for all the effort.

The Rector cranked up, softly, at first, then increasing slowly to awake those snoozing or likely to be. Usually, it was not hell and brimstone, leaving that to the Baptists or Fundamentalists. These Episcopalians referred to by others as Whiskeypalians, were independent, determined and able to avoid the reaches of the Baptists and the Catholics. This religion was a continuation of the Anglican movement, begun by the British in the 16th Century. After the Revolutionary War, to scrub society of the English influence, the Episcopalian title was substituted for the Anglican one. Another curve ball for the parishioners, was the institution of tithes, as the British had funded their churches from the public treasury. Pews were an exception as they were similar to rentals; one had their sole possession IF the tariff was paid regularly. Those British were certainly different.

Church was pleasant; many spoke to Morgan, especially the men, single and married; the latter while their wives' eyes were elsewhere. Finally working thru the crowd, they decided to go for a brunch. But where? There were a couple of Sunday restaurants, specializing in 'church' crowds; one, The Cupboard, had booths and no buffet; just a la carte. What they desired, order as you like, as much or little as suits you. Scanning the menu, both selected baked chicken and salad and a baked potato. Morgan drank water known to be better with meals; Gene endorsed that. The place was bright and cheery; the food was good and the company was special. Afterward, Gene drove around for some time; Morgan "Gene, I need to do some work at the house; I'll call you tomorrow". Gene "yes, please do".

At home, Morgan called Bud's parents to find out if they had heard from him; they asked her to come over; she agreed. Soon, she drove into the front; went to the door, opened before she got there. His Dad was standing there "Morgan, I hope that I didn't seem cryptic on the phone but Bud's OK". Morgan "did something happen?" Dad "yes, it was close to him, wounding him slightly, however, he's back at duty now". Morgan "thank goodness, what a scare". Mom "you're so right, our nerves are shot from this incident AND his overseas service". They chatted for a few minutes as Morgan tried to comfort them and ease their negative thoughts. She did a fine job on both. Morgan excused herself and departed for her home.

The rest of the day was spent writing a letter to Bud; she wrote about local news and then about the decision on Dave; she couldn't decide to bring up Gene, then reversed her decision; laying it out for Bud. Morgan certainly didn't want Bud to think that she was just flighty or fickle. She did say that Gene was an adult pupil of hers; in law enforcement. She hadn't heard from Bud in some time; now she knew why. She needed to write more often; that was her new resolution; don't forget it. Morgan, with time, went through her closets, extracting her post-college apparel, with various hemline lengths, 2 inches below the knee, 2 "above to 5 "above to the midi, almost showing her panties. The latter wouldn't be too bad if they were colored.

She was such a busy lady that afternoon that she searched for things to do; after that, she checked her towels and if worn in the least or with any small hole; they go to the homeless shelter. One of the 'youngsters called her to plan the next social, in two weeks; If the crowd wasn't too large, Morgan could have it at her house. Put it on hold. She then called her Mom and Dad to see if it was convenient for her to come over. It was AOK. They were waiting for Morgan; she had not been there for more than a week; it was like she had not been for some time; close families are like that. They were not aware of Gene, although they knew that Dave was at Plant Vogtle; Morgan had not informed them of their' estrangement but did now. They were not so surprised; this modern group moved either towards the altar or towards someone else. No lost time for these millennials.

All three chatted about the local news and Morgan told them about Bud's experiences; all were nervous about his safety and wished for the safe return of the unit. They knew not about Gene so she leaked it out, slowly. There was no surprise for them; she was 29, a mature woman, capable of making up her mind by herself. Nice thinking.

She was there an hour, then returned to HER home.

CHAPTER XV: LIFE SOURS

School started as usual, regular as the Moon appears; Morgan could do it blindfolded, as she had repeated these lessons over and over. However, she was not bored; she enjoyed teaching different classes, watching them learn and advance into more complicated matters. The pre-school and some of the faculty extra duties did not endear themselves to her, BUT she did her job well. Gene tried to be busy when she was in pre-school as he knew her hands were full; she did not need any extra concern.

The students were there the 1st Monday in September; ready to take on their classes. Only a couple of new teachers to replace those retired; her Senior class was about 40 in each group, about the right size for effective teaching. She knew only a few; there were more girls than boys, as usual; maybe half of each section were rural and the balance from the town, Morgan was pleased with her groups and anxious to get started. There were new history books, just warmed over, covering the period through the 'Cold War', the 1980s. Football was starting and she had the duty at the stadium the first game, likely selling tickets.

Friday came and Morgan had the duty in the ticket cage. She was busy, barely looking up when she sensed someone eyeing her; she raised her head, spying that Bud from the farm and pecan orchard; he strolled over as a peacock, saying" Teach, another year, you still look good; how's your boyfriend?" Morgan "Bud, you need to go in if you have a ticket; if not, we have a few left". Bud" I have one, thank you". Morgan" I'm busy Bud, just go on in". Morgan steamed 'that bearded, insolent creature has a lot to do'. 'He is a regular bas d.'

He was getting bolder, she thought; not breaking the law but violating society's rules. She couldn't do anything unless he got bolder and made a mistake. Morgan said nothing to Gene about this boy, as she guessed that he could be dangerous. She put it out of her mind, concentrating on her duties. She planned to call Dave when she got home; she didn't know what to say but thought that it might be over between them. And he might be of the same opinion; Morgan was sure that in that rural area, there were many good, educated girls. Dave was not the type to let the grass grow under his feet and might already have a girl or two. They talked about everything but the subject; but it was hemming each in; Morgan took the bull by his nostrils "Dave, it's not working and I think we might consider throwing in the towel; what do you think?" Dave "Morgan, it takes two to play Honeymoon Bridge; you are smarter than I am; we've had a great run AND I won't end it on a bad note; I wish you the best, Goodbye". She'd just stared at the phone but he was right; only Jesus could resurrect something dead, and this was deceased. First, she felt numb but, a bit later, she was glad about the ending. She was free to date Gene or whoever asked her. She slept well that night.

The Fall sped by, the trees shedding their leaves, giving the sun a chance to shine through, warming the spots touched by the sun. Morgan was on a steady course, rarely being touched by feelings of inadequacy or insecurity. She took a day at a time, what most deep thinkers recommend; Gene seemed to be as congenial as ever; he was caring, attentive and understanding. He knew about Dave, but was impartial; not all concerned about her connection to Dave.She was busy but the weekends made up for the school loads. Her WCC classes just rolled along; no grade except P or F, the latter rarely given and in the most unusual circumstances. These were men needing every minute of this instruction: and she saw that it was delivered. Her banner never flew so high as when she was engrossed in teaching them the multitude of brain or personality disorders frequently found in suspects/offenders. Would each remember the details of the disturbed offender's diagnosis; not likely, but the characteristics would be familiar. A good deal is when both parties are satisfied and these 2 were.

Morgan, the thinker and philosopher, was the prime mover in the teaching profession; always searching for better methods of improving the reception as well as the delivery. Her results while not documented, in the records, were reflected in students' performances. Even Ps and Fs may have, for some a plus and for the others, Fs might be a wakeup.

She and Gene were beginning to be paired in the public's eye; there was only one concern; would he progress with her without her leading? And what would she do when and if, the 'moment' arrived. She knew from her history that her affection in an involvement could and might lead to a physical melding. Was that bad? She felt not necessarily, if 2 feel strongly about one another. He had not approached her about sex BUT it had to occur soon. The offer, that is.

Morgan knew that she could control her emotions and hoped that Gene could; but where do dating adults go after months of dating and kissing; perhaps a bit of feeling but no contact between their intimates. Probably the average cycles as between most dating couples, if there existed any standards for sexual matters, the time before they actually did it, might be 6-9 months..

This item was briefly covered in the Psychology book, not reflecting that one's emotions rather than the intellect, was the driver of the race to the bedroom. Are there actually conversations about the odds of a melding and, if so, at what point in the relationship? In fact, not a great deal of intellect is inserted by the lechers, whose emotions contribute to all speculation. These stabs at the possibilities of two very close parties exposing themselves totally to each other are, to me, mysteries.

Morgan, busy as she was, did wonder about the happening, but in a more mature and romantic sense. In fact, she was, not frequently, engaged in a self-analysis, using this as a springboard to her possibility of submitting to the entreaties of her current swain. She spent some time examining his physical attributes, concerned that she was not attracting him to the honey; was he too much of a gentleman to sally forth to a coupling? Is the natural consequence of closeness of a pair as described? Not easy to phrase or answer with any accuracy, so where does this lead? Like a circle without an exit.

The Fall quarter was moving, the holiday break imminent, all anxious. Morgan and Gene had not discussed their plans for these days, however, she usually hung around the area, visiting some folks, sending cards, maybe calling her sister, Marsha. If she and Wayne, the silent one, were not coming down, changes were necessary. The exchange with them was a long-ago ritual, not useful on today's rapid track.. Mom and Dad and Gene were her concerns for Christmas; she had these in her sights for solely practical gifts. Oops, she forgot the 'youngsters' club; one for either sex not exceeding $12 including tax.

Gene came over one chilly day, and they made themselves plan somewhat their schedules for this period, including New Year's Ball at the Elks' Lodge, big band, large crowd, the works and a must. Then Christmas morn, at her Parents' house; the afternoon at a charity tea at the Library. She couldn't miss the charity boxing, filling of presents for a number of children, who would have nothing without this project. Then she left time for Gene and herself.

A call came from Bud's parents "Bud was coming home by 24 December 2004," Morgan rushed over to express her joy with them; they were ecstatic, beside themselves; a number had already come home, in sealed boxes. Was this gruesome selection preordained, or just happenstance? There were advocates for both views; was the reason for the survival of many based on 'a necessity for the chosen to perform further deeds in life? The Presbyterians said no but the other religions were not so sure. The answer is that there is no answer.

Morgan felt much better after the news of the 'boys' coming home; in a small town, the Guard is an integral part of the area; composed of those 18 to 38 and up. The high school boys were eager to join for the excitement and the small check at the end of the month PLUS the 15 days summer camp; a time for hanging out with the boys. But when the bugle blew for the Middle East conflict, a bit of enjoyment declined. However, as time elapsed, the troops came to appreciate their roles in preserving or initiating Democracy.

Time passes swiftly in mid-December, and Morgan bought her presents early, for the first time in years. The only trouble was Gene's present; Morgan liked him a lot but still had not seen his pad. Somehow, she thought that he had kept the condo from his marriage, but was unsure, Well, without information, she must go on general knowledge; it was between two choices; a shoe tree, only 3% of men had them; the other choice was a clothes 'tree' on which to hang his clothing; one 'tree' won out.

The gifts were exchanged, a light lunch was partaken and time was available; she/Gene decided to ride around for a time. While riding in the country, only on paved roads, she sat close to Gene, as a teenager clings to her 'man'. They rode near the 'creek' and suddenly, Morgan said "turn here into this narrow road; a secluded creek lies at its end."

Gene, never surprised by Morgan, did so, stopping at this 'sanctuary'. Morgan "I used to come here; it seemed to calm me and let me pretend about my future; I haven't been here lately". Gene listened, just reflecting on the moment. As he sat, gazing at the placid waters, Morgan kissed him. Gene was not all stone, as he returned the kiss and joining their torsos in the front seat. Their breaths began to quicken, Morgan" I wanted you to experience the magic of this place; it can be ours as our bonds firm up". Gene "I feel that both of us have faith that something good will evolve from our association and plan something in a month or so, perhaps Valentine's Day (or night). I want to please you and show my feelings by a tangible present".

Morgan was thinking 'what does he have in mind? Are we on the same wave length? Why does he speak like an undertaker?' He is not a game player so this must be 'R' day, a round, narrow band of gold, pledging his troth". Gene, gently cranked the car and headed back to their original route. Silence, but for once, both were on the same page.

On the way home, Morgan glanced at him, from the side of her eye; his look, serene, confidant and optimistic. She took on the aspects of his persona at this time. At home, she continued to diagnose the actions of both; satisfied that each was taking a step forward just as the other. Yes, she was beautiful and charming, but was his interest, true love?

It was not the end or the beginning of the end of their connection morphing into stability; as, Churchill said in 1940 to the British people, it was the end of the beginning. Morgan delved deeply into Gene's psyche, looking for the keys to his life. She had never dated anyone who resisted her charms for very long; he did not either but was slow, or cautious, about the complete surrender of his being to her charms. Was this not beneficial to both? Yes, logic says, but contrary to Morgan's experiences. The play goes on.

Back at school in the early days of 2005, things were like they were every January; the farmers had set new records from the 100acre spread to the 5000acre plantation; bumper crops, the rest of the world grasping for Georgia's farm abundances; the farmers putting this capital to work: new machinery, several joining to purchase the larger items; new seeds, fertilizer and irrigation equipment; all better than before. A new frock or two for Mom, a Fox double-barreled shotgun, the pride of hunters and a new (or almost) pickup. Morgan could see all these improvements just listening to the rural kids exchange information on their families.

The Senior class was bright, eager and prepared to face the balance of the year. They paid attention in class, something often missing in other groups. Their books, mostly, remained unmarked, indicating respect for the property of others. The Winters here were mild usually, rarely freezing; this was needed to kill off insects, bugs, etc. Some of the boys said that in those open fields, at times, the wind chill lowered the temperature; jackets were in order.

She and Gene were together more in January; not necessarily going 'out' but being at her house or his condo, she finally getting in to view it. Pristine, orderly and immaculate were descriptive of this dwelling; he had a large 4 poster bed, with NO canopy over it. His suits were uniform, all buttoned, facing the same way with 21/2 fingers between his hangers. How does one do 21/2 of anything? But it was. He tried nothing but Morgan was thinking of something to do with the bed; not a wish so much as some sign of his virility. Not yet.

At her house, Gene was protective of her privacy and her reputation; nothing to give anyone, any hen of Prosperity, any room for cackling out gossip. They were almost as a married duo in their actions, vis a vis each other AND the outsiders. He was a reader, an amateur philosopher, almost a mystic, at times; he gave Morgan a start at times, by reading her mind on various topics. When would each quit this psychoanalyzing?

Time flew during the holidays as all were polite to the others, but only until January 2d, when all habits returned; school almost seemed as a relief, after the hurry up of the holidays. Of course, one had to 'admire' the new autos, trucks, 4 wheelers and every vehicle, that man could devise. The one positive, was that all had renewed energy to tackle the Winter quarter; and not spent what we had not. Another banner year for the farmers; with the irrigation systems, they could weather almost any conditions except hail or tornados. Hail was usually unexpected and deadly, to plants, animals and machines. It was some expense but crop insurance was the wiser move; one just could not afford to bear the cost of damages from these natural calamities.

Morgan and Gene were still entwined but not intimate; unlikely that anyone thought of their physical relationship. Morgan "was Gene impaired in some way or did his religion, whatever it is, prohibit sex before marriage?" Why did she omit that he was considerate of her, desiring that she make the move? But that is ridiculous; the man always moves first, doesn't he? Morgan said to herself "this is silly, just let nature take its course; to interfere with nature's order might not be best". Quit it, Morgan.

In January, February and March, she and Gene were constantly together, at his condo or her home. He did his 'homework' and she evaluated her students; he was still enrolled in the CC. Around the first week in January, Bud, her friend arrived home from those deserts of the Middle East; Morgan being at his home to greet him; he was tanned, slim and handsome in his Sgt's uniform. He said that they were 'standing down', had been promised that they would not be redeployed until 6 months had passed, if even then. His plans were, if possible, to open his accounting firm in Prosperity. All thought that this was a great idea. Bud seemed settled, very mature and reflective on life; a very nice person. Morgan told Gene about these events, and he nodded and smiled.

Her schedule was still crowded, but the young club in Prosperity, still met at least once a month; the February gathering was a fish fry at someone's 'mill pond', plenty of outdoors and water. No dancing but lots of fun, eating and enjoyment of nature. Heading back around 9:45, Gene pulled just off the main road, out of sight.

Morgan" is it a flat tire or do you want to kiss me?" Gene" the latter, I think". She" are you sure?" Gene just nodded, with a strange look on his face "Morgan, I really respect you and don't want to do anything to cause you trouble". Morgan" what do you mean?" Gene" I like your kisses and would want to go further, however, you have an important position in this town; it's important that you maintain the respect of all". She leaned over, holding his head as she kissed him with a long buss. Gene sighed" that was so good I might have to ask for another". Morgan" you can have seconds and thirds, if you desire". Gene nodded like a Christmas doll. It was getting late and he walked her to the door, holding her like an egg. Then she turned at the same time as Gene; their lips met in a repetition of a bit earlier; her bright lipstick was on his lips and face but he was content with it. They whispered goodnight and he drove away. Morgan thought" he does care for me; he's likely one of three men in this county to hold back on getting to me".

Morgan was pleased with his response; he cared for more than just tasting her sweets. That is love, thought Morgan; I'm not bringing that up again. She was not worried about his manhood or his being overly aggressive. That night, she slept well; no dreams but lollipops as the tykes said. She went to church by herself, enjoying Sunday School with its socializing and the sermon, deeper into the New Testament. Greeting all, after it concluded, she headed for her parents' home to visit awhile; spying their car in the driveway, she pulled in. They heard her car so both came out the kitchen door; they greeted her from their spots. Morgan exited her car, walked fast to their location, and hugged both. Mother "Morgan we're having a bite; please join us". All went into the kitchen and talked as they had a sandwich. She brought them up on her latest, mentioning Gene in the process; she could tell that they liked him; Morgan talked about her two teaching jobs; their delights and, at times, their headaches. They nodded as if these were the biggest problems in Prosperity. More conversation; then Morgan" I have to go to complete my lessons plan for this week; I'll see you before next weekend"

. She did work the rest of day on her classes' issues. She felt as Sunday was a special day and any work should be light and necessary. And Monday was usually a day of surprises, so careful preparation was essential to an orderly presentation of her materials. Morgan was superb at rationalizing possible snags and, how to avoid these by early and proper attentions to details.

Morgan was in the prime of life; healthy, self-supporting, great family, two wonderful teaching opportunities; a nice boyfriend; her own life, house and car. She was not one to brag but as she evaluated everything; she recognized that being married with children was her acchilles heel or perhaps just fate. Why couldn't she realize the benefits that so many other women, not as blessed as her, are enjoying each day? She knew that she was not alone in her intense desire to produce her own family, but she felt isolated. She was aware of Psychiatrists' general recommendations, in cases of emotional disturbances, to talk about recurring matters; it didn't work for her; was the apple too distant from her reach?

Morgan, shaking the weight off her, plunged into her activities with abandon; a strong and capable lady, perhaps a Princess but not yet the Queen. On Monday, she returned to her fortress, the classroom, where she was, in reality, in her vogue; teaching the diligent, molding their characters and observing their intellectual growth.

Though January, into February, the girls hyped up a Valentine's Prom, not formal, but classy. This idea and its conclusion were solely by students; the faculty encouraged them and assisted. It was a coat and tie affair, so many swains were forced to let their fathers or mothers tie their neck pieces as they had neglected that art. On 14 February 2005, the event was initiated. The school was furnishing chaperones and monitors; Morgan at the head of the list; she and Gene would be at the entrance, checking on attire and the status of the attendees, to inquire if they were students or dates of students.

She and Gene were there early, insuring the gym was in shape for this event; they had 30 minutes to go; a pickup pulled up, a bearded man emerged. Morgan looked and "Gene, it's Bud Crabapple, my former student". Bud "Teach, can I come tonight?". M "yes, Bud if you have a date who's a student plus a coat and tie". Bud "I don't have those". M "you have time to collect them; it doesn't start till 8P". Bud "I'll take a raincheck on it". He returned to the pickup and spun out of the lane, dust flying. Gene "he should be a crop duster".

The dance went off successfully with 76 great students taking part. Mogan and Gene helped secure the gym, then went their way. At her house, Gene gave her a Jade necklace instead of flowers and her surprise was genuine; with her skin coloring, this was the icing on the cake. Gene was working at a project so he left. Her cell phone rang, it was her Bud (Carter) "Morgan, I need to talk to you, tonight if possible". Morgan "come on over Bud". He arrived shortly, entered and said "Morgan you're so great, seeing me this late". Morgan "Bud, you're like family; what's on your mind?". Bud "first things first, Morgan, I can't get you out of my mind". Morgan "it's been some time for us, are you sure?" B "in combat, things are a lot clearer; what you thought was your career pattern, seems bleak without a partner". Morgan "you realize that we've gone separate ways these past two years?". B "yes, but you were never out of my thoughts". M "nor you out of mine". Nobody blinked as they sat on the couch, Bud taking her gently into his arms, then kissing her with tenderness; Morgan responded automatically. They went for seconds; finally coming up, just staring at one another. Morgan "you know that I'm seeing someone?". Bud "I know but I can't stop until we have another chance". Morgan "a few rules, Bud; this has to be quiet, at least until Gene and I make a decision; that means no public appearances at this time and no telling anyone". Bud "I agree; now it's late so I'm going". A quick kiss then he was gone in a flash.

This arrangement continued for just 3 weeks or so when, Bud called one afternoon "Morgan, we've been alerted to leave within 3 days for the Middle East, Engineer outfits were scarce and our expertise is needed now". Morgan thought "he's going back into Death Valley; I have to see him tonight." She had an early class at WCC; he could pick her up afterwards; at 8P she had finished and he was waiting outside; neither wanted to eat; they just wanted to talk. He drove out to the Airport, only used in daylight; there was a road all the way around the runways with little pathways into the trees. He drove out of sight. Then he turned to her as she sat close; both expectant about the present. Kissing her, her breast came into contact with his hand. It was so soft and pliable, that Bud had to kiss it. Morgan was breathing heavily as if she had exerted herself; she was helpless as they moved slowly but steadily towards some further closeness. Afterwards, Morgan "Bud, I haven't had anything like that, I assure you." She had told herself many times NOT to become involved with Bud Carter but her will melted.

They only spoke on the phone 3 times before his unit shipped out. Morgan was blue for days; Gene observed that, asking her "what's the matter Morgan?" She "maybe the weather or school, I don't know". He was satisfied and she just sighed. She never wanted him to find out about Bud; that would chill it. She was caught in a dilemma now; Gene was a regular guy but she was gradually concluding that they were not suited for the long haul. Was it really Bud after all; Dave and Gene and maybe now she really wanted to date someone else? Here she was, Morgan thought '30 years old, well educated, pretty, talented, BUT still not with that so important ring on the 3rd finger, left hand; why not?' Again, she acted like Scarlett in 'GONE WITH THE WIND', as she said to herself "I'll just worry about that tomorrow". And she did, but not much.

Morgan knew that she'd write Bud or better, make a tape for him; at least every week if not more often. How does she break up with Gene? Morgan was soft hearted and breaking up for her was not easy. The best way was to tell him about Bud but, she knew, that wouldn't go so well around Prosperity or SW Georgia. Maybe it would work itself out and maybe her pumpkin would turn into a carriage. Just maybe.

CHAPTER XVI:
FALL or 'THE 'FALL'

Entering October 2005, a beautiful time of the year, with the hardwoods beginning to turn their leaves; the money-making trees; the pines, losing some needles but maintaining their dull colors, were often the saviors of the farmers. They could be cut every 20 years, but by increments; almost every 5 years. The imports of Canadian timber hurt the prices for the small farmer, who needed top dollar for his fewer trees. This time of the year was invigorating with the farming kids sponsoring cane grindings, peanut boilings, hayrides and barn dances; ushering the town students into the rural community.

Morgan was into the first quarter; with finals due the third week of October; She was a fixture at the basketball games, often selling tickets. One night she spotted Bud Crabapple, on the outside with his sidekick, J.D. Wright. Morgan to herself "I know that Neanderthal, with his smirk, will come over here". He did, grinning like Willard Clutchmeyer, "hi, Teach, good to see ya". Morgan only nodded 'he was getting bolder and it looked more muscular' thought Morgan. She only said to him "Bud, I'm only selling tickets, do you and J.D. want a couple?" Bud "only if you go inside with me". Morgan, steaming "only when you grow up". Bud turned and exited the premises, scratching off with his hopped-up Ford pickup, throwing dust everywhere. Morgan thought 'that boy is trouble with a capital T; why doesn't the Army get him?" This was a fleeting thought as her mind shifted to her man, Bud, in danger 24/7 in the sands of the Middle East.

With Morgan's mind on her Bud in Afghanistan, Gene began to accuse her of 'daydreaming' but he knew not of what. She was writing Bud constantly; when it came from the blue "we're on the way home; be there by 18 October". Now Morgan had to break it to Gene and she did, "Gene, I didn't plan it but my relationship with Bud has grown; he's coming home around 18 Oct and I plan to meet him". Gene stuttered as he had difficulty forming words "Morgan, this is out of the sky; you must be confused". Morgan "not so Gene; I couldn't help it; our relationship goes so deep that I had to follow my heart". Gene couldn't respond, saying meekly "Morgan I'm giving you a few days to clear your head; I'll be in touch". She felt terrible BUT what was better? Not telling him?" He departed and would likely not be back.

Morgan just threw herself into her work as well as social events by the 'Young Club" in this Autumn. The leaves had turned with the hardwoods in the woods adding such a variety of colors to a usually drab landscape; just biding time until Bud came home. Did she love him? Wow, she hoped so, burning her bridges behind her. The thought occurred "what if Bud didn't feel the same?" 'He HAD to; this was the time to fish instead of bait the hook', thought Morgan.

The 'gang' knew at once that something was different as Morgan showed up 'stag' at their functions. Morgan said zip about Gene, focusing on Bud's return home. It was nice to be able to converse about Bud, the first love of her life; she did reveal a few items that Bud had conveyed to her about the conditions overseas. Before Morgan knew it, the time was here; Bud was in the States, en route to Atlanta with a transfer there to Macon. His parents were picking him up there AND Morgan planned to be there also.

She called his parents and they were overjoyed about her wanting to go. ETA at Macon was 5:30P, not quite dark but approaching twilight. They arrived early in a spot to spot the incoming flights, not that many for Macon. Soon, it landed, slowing to the EXIT ramp. The passengers left the plane, one soldier stood out, tall, muscled, decorated in khakis and a beret. Bud was home. On the way home, Morgan held her tongue as the parents drilled him with questions about a multitude of subjects. He and Morgan held hands in the back seat as teenagers do, both so excited over the moment. The ride was over so quickly as they let Morgan out. Bud was still in the time zone exactly 12 hours ahead of EST; it was now AM tomorrow in the Middle East. She kissed Bud and said she'd be here when he had rested; he nodded.

In her house, as she prepared for bed, she had many thoughts in her head as she reviewed the events of today; seeing Bud in his uniform, tanned and leaner than she had remembered, stirred up something in her that she thought was dead. Bud was her first and now, hopefully, was her last. What was her future? She wanted to be a Principal at some time but her future was entwined with Bud's; wherever he went, she would go.

On 19 Oct 2005. Bud called her at school around Noon, wanting to see her after school at her home. She agreed as she rushed through the last hour, outlining the homework for the weekend. Morgan left when the bell rang driving straight home; the week was hard but not impossible. She changed clothes to something casual, the weather was still warm so a skirt and blouse would do. Shortly, Bud rode up, parking behind her car. He got out to view her 'digs' as he hadn't seen her house before. They chatted for a minute, then Bud asked Morgan to take a ride. Morgan "I thought that you'd never ask?" Bud "woman you talk too much". Morgan "Yes, Sergeant". Bud "soon to be civilian Bud". M "Bud what are our plans for now?" B "I'll tell you on the ride".

They rode for some minutes when Morgan began to recognize certain areas that she'd seen before. Bud slowed down, turned right onto an unpaved path with trees right up to the edges of the road. He pulled up at the old place, cutting the car off. He reached for her and she slid into his embrace; they kissed and all of a sudden, the temperature went up for both. Bud, raised her skirt revealing two tanned and shapely legs, joining at the thighs with a wisp of lace between them. A sight to behold. Morgan "Bud, before we begin anything, we need to make some concrete plans for the future". Bud "Morgan, you're right; you need to have a man that is settled down or soon to be so; the combat has confused my mind and really upset any plans that I had. Can you give me a few days to clear all this up and we can decide our futures together. .

They talked as they drove around before taking Morgan home; Bud had a multitude of things to do for the next week, outlining his plans for civilian life. Morgan had her 'finals' due for Friday, 21 Oct 05. She eased through those, looking forward to a nice weekend. Her phone rang as she opened the door, asking her to assist with a beauty pageant on Saturday afternoon and attend a barbecue of a school official that night; Morgan loved the pageants and looked forward to seeing friends at the cookout. They usually did the old fashioned 'barbecue' complete with a pit covered by wire, barbecuing a whole hog over a number of hours. A big fire to make the coals, moved under the wire to the bottom of the pit, to cook the meat slowly and thoroughly. Nothing like it; if it was good enough for their Grandads, it was fine for them.

The pageant was fairly local, with 3 other counties included to each a reasonable number of contestants, as no small town in that area could supply more than 2-3 ladies; even Prosperity with its 'lookers' from town and farm. The talent part was the most difficult plateau; what were the possibilities? Piano, fading out, twirling, only for the young, reading, boring; what's left?. Athletics weren't included, eliminating a number of talents. Science was a possibility but the Judges didn't favor brains; they beauty and raw talent.

On Saturday, she ran her errands early, appearing at the pageant in Sylvester around 4:30PM; they had 22 girls vying for the title of Miss I-75; all pretty and hopeful. Morgan assisted in configuring the hair of some, helping some 'put on' their makeup and, handling last minute issues, I.e. a button off the dress, a corsage that didn't pin properly or minor tailoring needs of the girls. Their dresses were pretty, not expensive, or flashy; but suitable for this contest. For those who would go further, a new 'frock' was in each's future. As in all the preliminary events, there were cuts; the first cutting at least a third; the second cut a third and the final cut was down to five contestants. Then the selections could take several 'entries' of each, finalizing with a 5th and 4th place winners; then the finale of the 3rd, 2d and winner. It sounds quick but when each has a talent to display; it takes 3-3/12 hours. Over at 8P, Morgan headed for the barbecue, not far away. She saw many friends and a number from Prosperity; they chatted, each asking her "when?" Morgan was vague but did offer that she was not going with anyone 'steady' but Bud was home for good. Enough said. Seeing all her friends consumed a couple of hours, so she slipped away quietly around 10:30P; stopping at another friend's house for a few minutes. Then she went home as it had been a long day.

Morgan was not at Church the next morning but this was not unusual as she often worked on pageants out of town, arriving home late at night. Her car was under her carport and house appeared normal. Sunday passed and Monday AM for school; Morgan wasn't there and some official called the Chief of Police to check her house. He did, found it locked, her cellphone in the car; he forced entry, discovering several items out of place, a lamp overturned, the headboard broken on the bed, her clothes of the evening lying around and a bed support broken. These factors indicated to a trained investigator that there had been a struggle, beginning or ending on the bed as some fairly large weight had broken the bed.

The Police called the Georgia Bureau of Investigation as this was not just a normal break-in. Their personnel, including a lab man, arrived that afternoon, assuming jurisdiction over these matters. A purview of a close dempster revealed a lady's purse and set of keys to the auto and the house. There was the card from a policeman stuck in her front door asking her to call and a physician's glove lying on the front lawn; DNA was found in the house but was later found to not be a match in any database. Unless one has gov't service (the service, Civil Service,etc) or a criminal record, there can be no match. No fingerprints were retrieved. Other GBI agents arrived within days to begin the interviewing of all who knew Morgan, hoping for any scrap of evidence or indication of anything. They had assumed that this was a kidnapping and a few had opined that it was likely a 'snatch' by someone outside the area. Why, this 'thought' was beyond me. The GBI had a fairly good reputation at this time as perceived by the public. Only time would validate or decry this opinion. They did let leak out their theory(really?) of the crime; but why and about the money (little); it was initiated by so many or one who were seeking money. Yes, try a schoolteacher if you want to rob and get $200. Wow; this was concocted by some great wizard of their Headquarters; how about the taking of the best -looking lady in SW Georgia; was this just for money? When there was $200 in her car's console? No, my friend, it was about the other motive for crime, after money and revenge.

Morgan had some other law enforcement friends, including the one whose personal card was found in her front door; several of the agents began Interviewing these, to include her students at Worth Community

College; you know how this goes, agent asks "do you know anyone else who knows her?" It broadened out to include anyone that she had dated within 5 years or so. Naturally, her former students at WCC were interviewed, including Gene. Lots of talk but no evidence at all.

The house and car had been thoroughly examined and the driver's seat had been moved forward; the cat was OK but unable to talk. The interviews took time but the evidence was very sparse. Morgan's sister came down from Augusta to be with the parents. Nobody knew nothing as the saying goes; or if they did, their lips were sealed.

The town of Prosperity was aflame with rumors, fear and wonderment; nothing close to this had happened anywhere in this area of Georgia before; what was the answer? The GBI was close-lipped but that meant nothing since they had very little to show for their efforts. They were still following procedures, many of which were outdated; they might have sought the assistance of an expert in these types of crimes but did not, as known to the public. One wonders why the Agency did not go to 'undercover' agents around Prosperity to mingle in with the locals JUST in case their theories were incorrect. You know of course that no evidence or even information is released by the GBI until the investigation is completed, whether it takes 2 months or 20 years. One joke going around was about the ex-agent who fell on hard times and robbed a bank, writing the note for the $$ on the back of his deposit slip. He got great training at the agency.

Everyone around the area had a conclusion, always wrong, about the background of this case and, gradually, the subject faded from view. Even with a reward for information leading to a conviction of the party responsible for Morgan's disappearance of 100K or more; no tangible tips came forth. Likely, a few 'full moon' observations emerged but, no cigars. All got used to seeing the 'stripped', allegedly, undercover agency autos around town, with the drivers arrayed in tie and coat, like insurance salesman. Not exactly impersonal or similar to the locals' stripped down, open mufflered pickups or hybrids. The agents were recognized about 200 yards away; their badges were superfluous on these jaunts. If you really wanted to cause a ruckus around their Headquarters, just call giving a tip about some white guy dozing in some vague colored Chrysler with Fulton Co. Plates on it. Wow; roast him.

Morgan's family was naturally destroyed by a lack of information as to her situation; a few held out hope that she might be alive; however, with no ransom notes or contacts by the underworld; her life appeared to be gone forever. The GBI did, I'm sure, work the case with their methods; there is no evidence that they experimented with various investigative techniques; the only way that this crime could be solved within several years. The news Media kept the matter alive by regular discussions of the circumstances surrounding the incidents; without them, it might never have been solved.

Time flowed as the river but Morgan was not forgotten; her friends, relatives and students continued to keep her situation vibrant and alive. Her friend, Bud, after his interview, continued his CPA career, always wondering about his first love. Gene, her prior friend, was more torn up about her mystery than any; her Mother died a few years later and her funeral was the largest ever held in Prosperity. Gene put up notices within 50-100 miles of Prosperity, about Morgan; praying that someone somewhere knew something. His broken heart doomed him to an early demise in 2011; just a few months after Morgan was declared legally dead in 2010. The ripples from the stone thrown into the lake, continue to seek more victims.

How many declared "I wish that I'd said more or I wish that I'd called her more". Her missing was a pall on many social events, or beauty pageants; it was difficult to enjoy these without Morgan. For a young lady of only 30, she had accomplished a great deal. Only questions; no answers; no echo when we shout her name. Innocence was beginning to disappear from rural SW Georgia

There was a pall over Prosperity and something else as the GBI found out quickly' the town folk gave no thoughts, suggestions, recalled very little and almost seemed to 'shut out' the investigation. Yes, it's not a crime to.fail to remember and the commission of a crime within a jurisdiction does not reflect on that area. But the lid was on their thoughts and conversations And the GBI couldn't crack this shell. It is unknown how many agents realized this problem but, it existed then and now. When seeking information on the incident, I ran into a stone wall with the newspaper and a couple of other knowledgeable parties, who could have been of great assistance. Time flew for some but was in reverse for others; the GBI still from time to time appeared and, to their credit, tried to follow every lead. There was a $100K reward for evidence leading to the conviction of anyone for the crime(s).

All who were associated with Morgan tried to get on with their lives but not so fast; this girl had made an impression on all who met her and this effect did not dissipate rapidly.

Around the first of February 2017, eleven years after her disappearance, a lady visited the Prosperity Chief of Police. He was cleaning out his files after the first of the year as she entered his small office. He greeted her familiarly, offering her a chair. In his friendly voice, "Betty Sue, what can I do for you? Is it J.D. again?" She could hardly speak but got out "no, not this time at least not totally". The Chief "just tell me the issue and we'll resolve it". BS "you remember Morgan, Morgan Mitchell, don't you?" Chief, swallowing hard, "you know that I do; what do you know?" Betty Sue "well, J.D. and Bud went to her house that night; Bud wanted to try to romance Morgan; J.D. told Bud that he was nuts but Bud did approach her anyway; she was less than pleased telling Bud "to get the hell out". "then Bud approached her trying to get her on the bed; he managed that; the ruckus broke the headboard and one of the side boards.

She slapped Bud, angering him and he grabbed her neck; she was fighting and trying to get away. Bud is strong and his hands got around her neck, breaking it". Chief "he killed her?" BS "according to J.D.; they panicked and put her body in Bud's truck, heading for the pecan orchard, owned by Bud's Uncle; they didn't know what to do so Bud (or JD) came up with the idea of burning her body to create problems in any autopsy. Bud had this oil barrel with the top cut out; they placed her in it and covered her with gasoline, igniting it, consuming her remains". Chief "let me get our secretary in here to type this up; you swear that J.D. told you this word for word?" Betty Sue nodded to this question.

It was like molten lava had been poured over the town; the Sheriff was notified; both suspects were quickly charged with murder et al; placed in jail and the GBI was notified. The Chief wanted to get rid of this hot potato NOW, as the statement was sworn to and signed by Betty Sue. Was it true? Who cared? Now the town had someone, two in fact, to beat on (just a metaphor) and the Chief could strut his stuff. It was like the Japanese had just surrendered on 9/9/45; if you were near a decent looking lady or even one that wasn't, you reached for her lips and whatever else was handy.

When the GBI trotted into town, you would think that they had arrested John Dillinger, Bonnie and Clyde all by themselves. They blew the dust out of their revolver barrels so that no one could accuse them of never firing the pistols except on the range. It was impossible to stuff all the law enforcement personnel into the courtroom who claimed a portion of solving these crimes. So why some questioned the natives, others tried to locate the remains; our suspects gave various locations including the pecan orchard. The agents kept a backhoe and a number of construction shovels busy for several days, following the confession of J.D. No remains there but exercise aplenty for the LEP. One wonders why they put so much stock in J.D.'s version of events, knowing his nose was growing by leaps and bounds. Anyway, no remains.

This case abounds oddities, a week or so later, both were arraigned in the courthouse for a number of charges, 3 felonies for Bud and a basketful of other, non-capital ones, for Mr. J.D., the pyromaniac. The female Judge determined that she'd put a 'gag' order on all, not just the parties but me or any spectators if we dared darken that door. The news media got on this and got the best hired gun on the First Amendment, David Hudson of Hull, Barrett of Augusta. The ink wasn't dry on her order before an appeal was on the way to the Georgia Court of Appeals. Eventually the Ga. Supreme Court nullified the order; we can talk about the case again.

Both parties are in Jail and the investigation continues. J.D. decided that since he had burped the details of the case over SW Georgia, he might as well 'cop' a plea, not exactly like 'cop' a feel. So, he did.

Both had attorneys, JD's appointed; Bud Southerland's barrister filed some 20 motions on his behalf; the premier one was to lower some statutes of limitation, because in the Fall of 2005, it was alleged that both the accused had been at a social gathering in the area, telling a few of the attendees what they had done to Morgan. Since no action was taken against either for this information; it was alleged that the local law enforcement had notice of it. The Defense theory was that there was a condonation of the events by the law leading to this motion to negate certain statutes/limitation on some charged offenses. In other words, this defendant should go free as he had spoken in public his guilt and no agency apparently wanted him. Full moon or what?

It's impossible to keep the GBI out of this as they control all the info and will not release anything or confirm any news report from any source about the matter of Morgan Mitchell. But as the FBI is finding out these days, there are dedicated employees who know that the public has certain rights also, provided that these do not jeopardize the investigation or national security. Two issues arose shortly after the charging of the two individuals with crimes against Morgan; one already discussed, contained in a brief for Bud, alleging statements by both in late 2005 regarding their complicity. This has not been verified to date.

The other is an interview of J.D. in the Fall of 2016 by an 'unidentified' GBI agent. This appears to have substance AS the GBI refused to acknowledge this or deny it in their responses to my FOIA or Open Records Request. Well, let's look at this; number one question is why interview Mr. Accessory regarding these crimes unless the Gibs had information on his complicity? It's easier to write Gibs than GBI, to clarify this. If they had info why let him go without a 'full sweat' or pants down spanking? Beats me but I'm not a Criminologist, just a longtime Prosecutor. To have one's claws on the evil one and not squeeze him, is, to most, almost criminal in itself. Yes, there may be some valid reasoning but if the Gibs can hold it from the public, we'll all be beyond needing it. Think on it. A hint of less than stellar competence by some members of the Prosecution and Defense. The DC for Bud was replaced; one opined to me "Bud has a new Lawyer". I responded with "no, Bud has a lawyer". Viewing briefs for both sides makes one wonder 'whatever happened to the spell check on the PC?" The current must not be sufficient in Sylvester to word process. It is not beyond comprehension that the Presiding Judge will throw some of those submitted legalisms back at the authors; to try to comprehend some of their offerings is like wrestling with the original Cherokee language before the Trail of Tears.

One wonders if BS had not sauntered into the Chief's office that February 2017 when would these crimes be solved? Likely when the working, assigned agents had retired, the investigative papers had yellowed and the two culprits had become Mayor of Prosperity and

Chairman of the County Commission. One opined "the GBI, can't be as inept as they seem". Oh, no. The latest is that the trial of Bud will be in September 2019 UNLESS he needs another delay. Rumor has it that his partner has 'rolled' and will testify against him.

The large question remaining even after J.D.'s confession is 'WHY' did this happen? Yes, the Gibs opined that it was about money; that's just a full moon guess. They're telling me that these necks risked their futures for a few bucks? No sir, this revolved around sex; Bud had an infatuation with Morgan and her disdain for him, in his twisted mind, translated to affection and desire. Morgan never gave him a thought beyond a half-cracked nobody. The saying is that a perception is to some, their reality. Add a six pack of Bud Lite and a Saturday night with no date and an explosive situation is created. Bud was aware of the sexual revolution and presumed that Morgan was as many others were; just coy. The bed being broken was proof of the struggle that went on. A bank robbery in daylight would make more sense. This neck may never mention this scenario but it's the only one that meets all the criteria. Will Bud come clean? Not likely as he'd rather walk on live coals for a mile than admit that ANY woman had rejected him. I can predict now that he will try every way that he can wiggle to 'trash' that girl's reputation.

One continues to wonder 'how can this set of circumstances meld together?' We have two failures, owners of two barstools at Zippy's, without any visible sign of gainful employment, advertising their complicity in several felonies, one a capital offense; chased (or not) by several hundred certified investigators, with a humongous laboratory and at least enough brainpower in their Headquarters to direct them to the right county. It seems that the broken headboard and broken support might have confused them; they thought that it was too early to cut fire wood. If a law enforcement agency in Georgia can ever be 'negligent' in a 'case' to the extent that their employer may be held responsible, economically and punitively, this is it. Their hold on the Open Records Act loosens at such a trial. A trial attorney's delight. Eleven years is a long time to suffer and justice would demand that some of the alleged professionals, be brought to the Bar to receive their just deserts.

Although some of the failures and oversights outlined herein, may seem to be fictions of an imagination or perhaps errors in the receipts of details of culpable acts; you may be assured that each action or failure of the Gibs occurred. It is not unusual for many organizations to try to shift the blame to subordinates; who are advised to document any orders or advice given to them; recording devices have many purposes. There is little that we can do for Morgan but, for her memory, we must seek that which is pristine, genuine and just, words used, at times, by some who don't understand them.

You know that when you have something in your mouth that is rancid or decayed, you must spit it out and; these words that fit this situation are often used without thought. It's interesting that when a governmental agency is engulfed by corruption, gross negligence or faulty memories; the fingers uplift to be directed towards another, usually lesser in rank, to take the 'fall'. Ever tried to catch a rat with a vaseline glove or an eel with a banana peeling? These are the reasons that most do not try to hold bureaucratic concoctions liable. But times are changing and the victims can now bite with a full set of molars; hanging on like a bulldog; even if one culprit is not financially ruined, his presence on the sturdy witness benches day after day, might ruin his fishing or the building of sand castles.

We've attempted to give the readers some education and a dab of pleasure by this work; we only represent the victim and her family. To progress towards a culmination of this undertaking, you were offered some insight into poor analyses, worse execution and an unconscionable delay of justice by those responsible for the identification of the guilty parties. What you do with these facts and how you use them is yours and yours alone. Evil cannot exist for long where the vigilant and concerned abide. For those who want to eliminate prisons, I recommend that they mentor and serve as Guardians at Litem for these buckaroos while housing them under their roofs.

K.G.WATSON

AUTHOR'S POSTSCRIPT

Bo Dukes, the associate of the confessed murderer in this case is being sought on warrants issued by Warner Robins for rape, aggravated sodomy and illegal detention of two females on 1/1/19. He was out of jail on a request-surrender agreement,living in Bonaire,Houston County,Ga. The result might be a certainty that he will tell the truth when testifying against his accomplice, Ryan Duke; his maximum sentence for all his offenses is in excess of 60 years. He already has a felony conviction for larceny from the US Gov't.

POST POSTSCRIPT

This issue raises its knarled head frequently in life or in fantasy whenever a beautiful lady, single or married, is the focus of any issue, a crime, tragedy or just a happening. SO is it here affecting or attempting to distort our narrative or recitation of the life of a successful lady. How does this occur? It is relatively simple; the propensity of males and a few females to dwell on the sexual aspects or possibilities of a lady who lives her life to the fullest with love, sorrow, disappointment without revealing each incident of her existence. With the emergence of the news 'blogs, it is not the truth that sears but some fantasy by a newscaster, reaching for fame by dragging a heroine through the mud. In this case, as outlined earlier, our victim had boyfriends and friend boys (can't the sexes just be friends?) and the town had, like small fiefdoms, a steady diatribe of gossip about any and all matters.

There are two incidents that stand out but are not supported by any evidence: the law enforcement officer who frequented her presence, calling some 15-18 times the initial weekend of her absence and placing his personal card in her door. The second is a former student, who allegedly had a 1 1/2 year romantic relationship with Morgan, being arrested one time while arguing with her in her yard. The names add nothing to our discussion. These and other facts make us wonder why Morgan stayed in this inferno of speculation and slander. A jab at it, not documented, is that she was not secure enough to go to cities; feeling more at ease around her parents and familiar people as well as the friendliness of a small Southwest Georgia farming community. Is that a crime?